"Are you trying to tell me they approve of Miss Needwood as a wife for me?"

"I think so. Mama does, anyway, which is the same thing. She said it were a great pity if you did not marry for love."

"Love? Who said I loved Miss Needwood?" cried Markham, conjuring up a picture of her as he had seen her the previous evening, holding on to Lord Veren's arm. "Love that . . . that . . . malevolent ingrate! I wouldn't marry her if she were the last woman on earth!"

"How agreeable that we are of one mind in that," said a hard voice from the doorway.

Looking up, Markham found himself looking into the vivid dark of Eleanor's unforgettable eyes. . . .

Also by Delia Ellis
Published by Fawcett Books:

A LADY OF BREEDING

PAINTED LADY

Delia Ellis

FAWCETT CREST • NEW YORK

A Fawcett Crest Book
Published by Ballantine Books
Copyright © 1994 by Delia Ellis

Library of Congress Catalog Card Number: 94-94658

ISBN 0-449-22358-2

Manufactured in the United States of America

First Edition: January 1995

10 9 8 7 6 5 4 3 2 1

CHAPTER

1

Propped on an elbow in the shade of an aged willow, Philip Arno, Viscount Markham, twitched the line with his free hand and concentrated his mind on the serious problem of angling. He enjoyed all sports, but angling was best, being the perfect way of pretending to be busy while doing nothing at all. Today the fish obliged handsomely by giving his line a wide berth, leaving him free to contemplate the taking of his luncheon of cold meats and fruit, lovingly arranged earlier by his manservant, beside him on the riverbank under a crisp white cloth.

His thoughts were on the bottle of champagne dangling by a string into the ice-cold stream, and he ruminated lazily on whether to fish it out and pop the cork. On reflection he rather thought not, and closed heavy eyelids against the world.

Drowsiness was becoming sleep, when he was all at once disturbed by the sound of a carriage being driven along the cindered track behind him, a modest roadway parallel to the stream that crossed his lands. He briefly debated the nice question of neighborliness, comforted himself with the thought that he was hidden by trees, and fell gratefully back into the vale of slumber.

He was jerked out of it by what sounded like a cry,

and was about to assume that he was mistaken, when the air was rent by several shrieks that had him springing to his feet. Still drowsy, he staggered through the tangled bushes onto the track and peered off into the direction of the sounds, confirming his fear that the carriage that had earlier disturbed him had come off the track. It was now perched half over the edge above the stream: Cursing quietly to himself, Markham hurried back to where his horse was tethered in the shade, climbed into the saddle, and cantered off toward the accident.

The carriage, an elderly barouche, had been carrying two ladies, and as he rode up he saw the younger clinging to the straps to stop herself from falling out while the carriage lurched drunkenly on the edge of the pathway. She was pale but stoic, and otherwise unhurt. It was from the other lady that the shrieks emanated, for she had actually been thrown from the carriage into the water, where she was now splashing about hysterically, while her coachman worked desperately to prevent the carriage sliding down the bank onto her. Reining in his horse, the viscount gentled him down the bank and into the water toward the struggling woman, calling hearteningly to her. Walking the horse out to the depths, Lord Markham leaned down, and with less concern for dignity than for life grabbed at the woman's skirts, which were billowing out behind her, dragging her inelegantly but efficiently into shallow waters. Having deposited her, coughing and choking, on the edge of the stream, he turned his attentions back to the carriage. Catching the leader's bridle, he soothed and quietened it, and soon righted the carriage, bringing it back onto the flat.

Glancing only long enough at the young lady in the

barouche to reassure himself that she was still calm, he grabbed a rug from the carriage and rode back to the other, who remained seated amid the boulders where he had left her. The feathers on her bonnet drooped miserably over her eyes as she cowered in the shallows.

"How are you now, madam?" he asked bracingly, fighting an unfortunate desire to laugh as he slipped down from his horse and threw down his rein.

"How the devil do you *think* I am?" she cried, resentful of the telltale tremor at the corner of his mouth. "How would *you* be if you'd just been dropped into a river by a ninny of a coachman?"

He had the grace to feel ashamed and, dropping the rug around her shoulders, made praiseworthy efforts to control his unfortunate sense of humor, while, with chattering teeth, the rescued lady continued with her tirade against the coachman.

"It's not entirely *his* fault, madam," said Markham, trying to be fair. "This stretch is notorious. Several strangers have come to grief here. Really it needs widening."

"I should think it does. It's a disgrace! Whoever owns it should be horsewhipped. I wish I had him here. I'd have something to say to him!"

"Then I suppose I must listen, for it's me you want. I own the road."

She stared doubtfully at the large, loose-limbed man before her.

"I am Markham," he explained with a shrug. "The lands about here are mine, so it's me you'll have to ring a peal over."

Shrewdly she looked him over, wondering if her first impression could possibly have misled her. His leather

jerkin and rolled-up sleeves had made her naturally assume that he was a local farmer, but now that she examined him more particularly, she could not help noticing
that his cambric shirt was fine and beautifully sewn,
and though he wore breeches and top boots, they, too,
were of the first quality. But his disheveled appearance
still puzzled her. In her experience gentlemen behaved
like gentlemen! And if he *was* Lord Markham, why was
he riding around in his shirtsleeves?

"I see you are wondering at seeing me in all my
dirt," he said, displaying the smile that had caused
many a heart to leap. "And indeed, it is shocking of me
to wander about in my shirt. But I was fishing, you see,
just a little farther on."

Quite inexplicably she knew he spoke the truth, and
her expression underwent considerable change. The
sourness drained away as if by magic, leaving the
smooth, ingratiating expression he knew so well and
heartily despised.

"My dear Viscount," she simpered. "What must you
be thinking of me? Here you are risking life and limb
for me and never so much as a thank-you. And the accident, too! Quite our own fault! We must have come
off the turnpike without realizing it. And my man,
pressing the horses much too fast! Do forgive me for
railing at you. You will be charitable, for sure, and put
it all down to alarm?"

Used to being toadeaten, he only smiled and put out
a hand to help her up.

"You are cold, madam. You and your traveling companion must come to the house to recover from your or-
deal," he said dutifully as he pulled her to her feet,
wishing her anywhere else. "You'll need to dry your-

self, and I am sure you will both like to rest before continuing on your way."

She threw him a coquettish smile that, since she was at least twenty years his senior, sat oddly on her plump shoulders. "Who would not be *charmed* at such an invitation, my lord?" she said archly, tactically removing her sodden gloves. "My daughter and myself will be more than grateful to accept your hospitality."

As she spoke, she put out her hand to him, obviously expecting him to kiss it, and since it was far easier to oblige with the old-fashioned courtesy than find a reason for not doing so, he touched it with his lips, though he could not help raising his eyes impatiently to the sky as he turned away. Too late he remembered her companion and, glancing over quickly, saw that she was peeping at him over the back of the carriage. She had seen the gesture, and her lips twitched appreciatively. Meeting her eyes, he shrugged his shoulders, and seeing it, her smile spread to include her eyes, which creased at the corners. Relieved that the girl chose not to be offended, he helped her mama into the carriage with exaggerated care, and with a word to the coachman to follow him, rode before them to the grange.

CHAPTER

2

Arno, a small two-story Gothic lodge set amid the Derbyshire hills, had once been a handsome little building and could be again, but that the present owner had allowed it to acquire a somewhat neglected air.

Nonetheless, glimpsing some fine fan-vaulted plasterwork as she passed through the entrance hall, Mrs. Needwood was so pleased with her introduction that she began to consider a wetting a small price to pay for it. Another woman would have become hysterical at being thrust into an icy stream: Mrs. Needwood wondered how it could be of use to her.

Lord Markham was less gratified, and while the Needwood ladies were being shown to one of his guest rooms to compose themselves, he grumbled at his housekeeper, summoned to prepare luncheon for his unexpected guests. Mrs. Tamsin had always been with the family and had rubbed bruised knees and kissed grazes better when he was a boy: Now she uttered soothing noises while he vented his spleen, something unusual for him, since he was good-natured to a fault and invariably too lazy to allow himself to be put out.

Today he had been touched on the raw: Not only had Mrs. Needwood deprived him of his fishing, but he recognized in her a woman it would be difficult to shake off.

"And the devil of it is, Tansy," said he, "she's precisely the style of woman who will pester me forever. It'll be just my luck to have her come up and claim me as the friend of her bosom when m'father's about, and then as well as telling me how lazy I am not to have mended the road, he'll start laying into me on the need to be more *particular* in my friendships, for you know what *he* is. And all because I fished the dashed woman out of the water instead of letting her drown. God, I hate encroaching females—"

He stopped abruptly, for Mrs. Tamsin had colored up and was staring fixedly past his shoulder. Following her eyes, he was dismayed to find the younger of the Needwood ladies standing just inside the doorway, having obviously overheard every word.

"Ah, Miss Needwood. There you are," he said with an attempt at nonchalance. "I wasn't expecting you down so soon."

"I thought you could not have been," she said gently, but seeing his cheeks redden, added hastily, "Oh, I'm sorry! It was unpardonable of me to tease you. She *is* an *encroaching female*, and I don't mind in the least that you should say so."

He stared. "Well, you should mind! I mean, er—not that I intended to suggest that—oh, I say!"

Her eyes widened. "Now you make me uncomfortable," she said with a slight pout. "It's hardly fair of you, when I'm doing my best to make you feel less embarrassed." Before he could say more, she said cheerfully, "I daresay you'll feel better if I explain that Mrs. Needwood is not really my mama at all, only my

7

stepmama. It will be that which accounts for the distressing lack of filial respect Papa charges me with."

"I know very little about such matters," he said dampeningly, "except that I am certain we should not be discussing her like this!"

"Should we not?" she answered easily and quite without rancor. "Then we won't. I was only trying to make you feel more comfortable."

He glared at her. "Shouldn't you be upstairs helping your mama? I can't imagine what made her allow you to come down alone, without her to chaperone you."

"Oh, I expect that is on account of your being a viscount," said Miss Needwood with disarming simplicity. "She probably wanted to give you a chance to flirt with me."

Startled, he raised his quizzing glass at her, a movement she accepted with perfect composure, observing simply, "I do wish you wouldn't do that! I do so hate being quizzed, don't you? Papa thinks it the height of bad manners."

Lord Markham, who rarely used the fashionable quizzing glass, blinked and allowed it to fall. In a voice devoid of expression he asked Miss Needwood to sit down. Placing himself on a chair close by, he began, with just the proper degree of reserve, to question her as to the object of her journey, determined to enter more usual channels of conversation. Miss Needwood dashed any such hopes.

"Mama and I are going to stay with Sir Maltby Tweede at the castle for a few days, my lord. Mama hopes to get him to marry me!"

Before he could stop himself, and to his distinct horror, he heard himself asking, "Isn't he rather old for

8

you?" a social solecism for which he could find absolutely no excuse. But Miss Needwood appeared to think his interest perfectly natural, replying with a naive burst of confidentiality.

"Well, he is, of course. He'd be too old even for *Mama*, besides being absolutely hateful! He drops snuff down the front of his shirt, and dribbles his wine! But he *is* a baronet, and there's no denying he's rich."

She saw that he was regarding her oddly, as though he required further enlightenment, and went on to explain. "Sir Maltby has the entree to the best society, or so Mama says. And if she's right, I suppose I have to try to marry him if I can."

"Is it so important that you meet the best society?" he asked, beginning to feel strangely interested.

"Not to me, but I suppose when you have a stepdaughter and three daughters of your own to marry off, with not very much money to do it, sir, as Mama has, it might take on a certain urgency. That's three besides me, you understand? It is the greatest affliction, as you may imagine."

"Yes, I quite see it must be. And so you are to be sacrificed?" She nodded. "And do you want to be sacrificed?"

"Hardly!" she replied with a confiding air. "But Mama is quite determined, so it's probably best to get it over with with as little fuss as possible."

Knowing how improper was their whole conversation, he yet could not help asking, "But what of your father? Why does he allow it?"

"Oh, I can't have Papa worried about such things!" she said briskly. "Papa is quite unable to stand up to Mama. She nags him, you see. Indeed, to be truthful, she nags us all. Dreadfully. Even my stepsisters. Her own daughters! None of us likes it much, but Papa cannot bear it. I have agreed to marry Sir Maltby only because Papa is quite worn out with quarreling, for you are not to be thinking I gave in without a struggle. I am not *so* poor spirited. But seeing how depressed Papa was, I was forced to agree. Mama doesn't shout, you understand? She is one of those infuriating people who whine. On and on, day after day, until we are all pleading to be allowed to do what she wanted us to do in the first place. And in my case, that's Sir Maltby."

"Isn't there anyone else you could marry? Someone younger?"

She thought for a moment. "There's Clary Ingram. He has wanted to marry me since he was ten."

"And is he eligible?"

"I *suppose* so. He is heir to the lands adjoining ours, and I know that Papa rather hoped at one time that we might make a match of it."

"Wouldn't that have been better for you?"

"Of course it would have, and though I can't say I ever *wanted* to marry him, I'd probably have agreed when it was put to me if I'd known that Mama would fix on Sir Maltby instead. And now that Sir Maltby seems interested, she won't hear of me throwing myself away on Clary. But I don't think I can be altogether blamed for not suspecting what would happen, whatever Clary says. Wanting to get married at Sir Maltby's age! It was hardly *likely*, now, was it?"

He considered her question rhetorical, and remained silent, feeling unaccountably depressed.

Miss Needwood, on the other hand, appeared to have brightened. "Of course, Sir Maltby *does* have an enormous appetite. And they say he drinks three bottles of wine a day!" she said, seeming to think this called for congratulations.

"I'm sorry? I—er—don't—"

"Well, he's already more than sixty, and with all that food and drink, I should hardly think he could live to a ripe old age, would you?"

Mentally reviewing his own family, he felt obliged to advise her not to raise her hopes too high, and was about to say so, when he recalled how improper was the conversation they had been having. Changing his tone considerably, he said in a hearty voice that even to his ears sounded much like his papa in one of his bumptious moods, "Tell me, Miss Needwood, what do you do with yourself when you are at home and not running about assisting your mama to fall into rivers?"

"All the usual things, sir," said Miss Needwood with a shrug of resignation that confidences were at an end. "I ride. I play tennis. Garden. And most days I teach my younger sisters in the schoolroom. Mama said we must dispense with the governess for being a perfect ninny, which I must confess she was—though perfectly good-natured! And I suppose I cannot altogether *blame* Mama for not wishing to waste any more money on bad governesses after it turned out that Miss McCranby did not even speak French properly, after promising in her letter that she was fluent in three languages! And when I am not teaching the girls, naturally I interest myself in the people on Papa's estate. As I say, sir, just the usual things. We are not very exciting at Evendale. And how do you spend *your* days, Lord Markham? What do *you* do?"

"Do?" He laughed, and leaned back against the cushions. "I'm not really called upon to *do* anything."

"But out of interest? What do you do to give your life purpose? Oh, what a silly question! A man in your position must have the most shocking demands on his time, I daresay. I imagine you are always being called on to settle disputes among the tenantry, and—and bring in improvements and matters of that kind, for I know Papa is, and your estate is far larger, isn't it?"

He smiled at her tolerantly. "Indeed, you make me sound quite a splendid fellow, Miss Needwood, but I must confess to having a man to do all that for me."

"You mean your land steward, of course, but they can't do what *you* can! And tenants like the personal touch, don't they? Papa says that any effort he makes in that direction is repaid tenfold by his tenants in loyalty, and that any man who leaves matters entirely to his steward is a fool."

"Does he, indeed?" said Lord Markham, flushing. "Yet I find *my* steward perfectly efficient. Perhaps your papa is not entirely conversant with matters on such a *large* estate as this one?"

"I should have thought that a larger estate would mean you needed to give it *more* time, not less," said Miss Needwood, wrinkling up her nose. "But I expect I have not perfectly explained myself. Mama is always saying I'm a gabble-merchant. I don't mean that I should expect you to be going about yourself collecting rents and things of that kind, which a steward is quite able to take care of. What I really meant, sir, is how do you interest yourself in the *lives* of your tenants? What do you *do* for them?"

"Why should I be called on to do *anything* for them? I assure you they are none of them in need."

"Why should you— What an odd question, to be sure. For certain they must be of concern to you?"

"I don't know that I've ever been accused of neglecting my tenants, Miss Needwood," he said, stiffening. "It seems to me that a *good* steward should be able to deal with *anything* that crops up. It's what he's paid for, after all!"

He would have said more but that a noise on the stairway heralded, at last, the arrival of Miss Needwood's mama, which on reflection was probably no bad thing, since Lord Markham felt that he had allowed himself to become ridiculously ruffled by a mere chit of a girl, a feeling that was not decreased by the fact that it echoed much of what his father was forever saying to him! He determined that Miss Needwood should be brought to see that there was enough difference in their spheres to account for his way of arranging matters, a lesson he wished his father might learn, and that he would begin himself by showing her that a gentleman of high degree would naturally be unaffected, and certainly unperturbed, by her contempt. She would not find him taking offence! At quite his most conciliating, he turned to welcome her mama.

Still a little damp about the hairline, but now attired in a smart carriage dress of gray Circassian, Mrs. Needwood glided into the room, her hand graciously outstretched to the viscount, who led her to a sofa, where she arrayed herself at an angle that enabled her to keep one eye on her daughter while she examined the viscount's furnishings.

Mrs. Needwood, now a plump, matronly figure, had

in her heyday been much admired. Though her flaxen hair was beginning to fade, and her chin, once round and neat, had now acquired altogether more substance, she could not rid herself of the illusion that she was still beautiful, and always entered a gentleman's presence with unshakable faith in her welcome. As she came through from the hallway, her self-esteem was so evident that Markham's chivalry was severely tested.

"My dear Lord Markham," she was saying in an ingratiating tone as she settled among the cushions. "What a charming house, and what a joy to have met you, even in such untoward circumstances. New friends are such a delight to me. I always say that friendship is one of life's most precious gifts, don't I, Eleanor, my dear?"

"Do you, Mama? I never heard you, but if you say you do . . ."

Mrs. Needwood eyed her daughter darkly but pursed her lips to the semblance of a smile. "Dear Eleanor. Such a tease!" she said sweetly.

Lord Markham could not rid himself of the conviction that Miss Needwood would later pay for her burst of candor, and rushed to fill the breach, suspecting that the girl would fare better if he proved tractable. Not quite understanding what made him want to assist Miss Needwood after she had been at such pains to make him uncomfortable, he yet found himself doing his best to put her mama into a sweeter humor. Seating himself beside her on the sofa, and with an indulgent eye on her stepdaughter (which he trusted would show Miss Needwood the superiority of his manners!), he ventured, with some hesitation, to mention the proposed visit to Sir Maltby Tweede, his nearby neighbor.

Mrs. Needwood narrowed her eyes. "What a little gabster dear Eleanor is, to be sure!" she said with a thin smile that chilled even Markham. He found himself hastily explaining that his had been the fault if Miss Needwood had been too candid.

Mrs. Needwood raised her hand as if to silence him. "How should you think I mind your knowing our destination? Yes indeed, sir. We are off to stay at the castle, with dear Sir Maltby."

She leaned forward with a confiding air that almost matched Eleanor's. "My stepdaughter won't have told you, but I think it would not be too *coming* of me to tell you that she has been fortunate enough to win the heart of that most amiable of gentlemen."

"Amiable? Ah, yes. Sir Maltby. Forgive me, I wasn't thinking. But yet, Sir Maltby Tweede. I'm surprised you are letting Miss Needwood go to him."

"Surprised? How so? He is a delightful man. So obliging. So distingué."

"Oblige?" he said with a terse laugh. "Shouldn't think he'll oblige you for one moment. It's common knowledge in these parts that he's clutch-fisted. He's never been known to spend so much as a sixpence where it could be saved."

"A young wife will change all that, Lord Markham," she replied without a sign of embarrassment. "Ladies have a way of handling such matters. He will dote on Eleanor, and what a life she will have! The London season! Brighton, I shouldn't wonder. And when her sisters come out, Eleanor will be in just the right company to chaperone them."

She appeared to be lost in an enchanted dream that Lord Markham set himself deliberately to dissolve. He had taken an intense dislike to the woman, and to see her sitting there so self-satisfied, deliberately planning a repellent marriage, was more than he could like.

"Oh, I strongly doubt that!" he reflected. "Tweede never leaves Derbyshire. He'll never stomach a London season. As for Brighton, it's out of the question."

Mrs. Needwood shrugged her plump shoulders. "Eleanor must change his mind," she said promptly. "It is a fine match and will put her in the way of being useful to her sisters." She lowered her voice confidentially. "Do you know, sir, I have been married to that girl's father for only a year and I've done more for her in that time than her father ever had. She is twenty, and had never even been to an assembly until I became her mama. Nothing but a few impromptu dances with friends. I leave you to wonder how she would ever have made an eligible connection had I not stirred myself."

"I always enjoyed the local dances, Mama," said Eleanor bluntly. "I am more comfortable dancing with people I know. And Papa is more concerned that I marry with affection than that I make a fine match!"

"Then it is foolish of him, Eleanor. Your papa means well, but he knows little of the world."

"Perhaps he just cares for different things—"

The viscount intervened. Smoothly, he dropped an idea into the conversation. "I'm surprised you don't give the girl a London season yourself, ma'am, if you want to do the best for her and for her sisters."

Mrs. Needwood pricked up her ears. "Naturally, that is the wish of my heart," she pronounced, turning her ingratiating smile back onto him. "But the expense! How could I possibly meet the expense?"

"There's no denying it would be costly. But worth it,

I'd say, for such a pretty little thing as Miss Need-wood."

"*Pretty little thing?* Eleanor? Oh, more than that, surely?" Mrs. Needwood said shrewdly, eyeing her stepdaughter with a proprietary stare.

And of course he *had* noticed that the girl was attractive, even when she had been annoying him. The ladies he commonly favored were rather more fashionable, but now that he came to consider the girl properly, he was certain that few men would find her anything but beautiful.

Looking her over dispassionately, he couldn't help thinking how grateful would be some he knew to exchange their own for Miss Needwood's sparkling good looks, and he found himself amused by the idea of unleashing her onto the ton. She had that certain something: probably to do with her eyes. Blue or gray eyes with her curling honey-colored hair, and she'd have been a beauty, but the dark, unexpected warmth of velvety-brown eyes, candid and open, made her something more. She had good skin, too, which gave her a look of health and vigor, and a tiny mole by her mouth that was surprisingly beguiling. Figure slender and trim, ankle well-turned, and if she only remembered not to jut out that determined little chin, and kept a guard on her tongue, both of which she would surely learn with a little town bronze, she must certainly be much admired. New clothes: a good town address: nothing simpler. He strongly reiterated his suggestion to Mrs. Needwood that this harum-scarum girl should get her London season, reflecting as he did so that, if nothing more, it would at least give her a few months more to try to land someone more suitable than Edwin Maltby Tweede.

"It would cost, but it must be money well spent," he said persuasively. "The girl's a diamond of the first water. Bound to take. Go to town in early March. Some of the best families are up by then, so she'd have time to find her feet before the crush in April and May. It's none of my business, but I reckon once she's acquired a little polish, she'll make a fine match. Plenty of men in town who'd make Tweede seem a pauper. And better-tempered men, too. No point in letting her go to the first bidder, is there?"

Mrs. Needwood sat lost in speculation. Her step-daughter—who by no means liked hearing herself considered a piece of property—charitably put down Lord Markham's unfortunate turn of phrase to a desire to make the proposition more attractive, and held her breath.

"But I know so few people in London, Lord Markham," whined Mrs. Needwood in the voice Eleanor knew so well. "I suppose you would not be willing—"

"You must not ask Lord Markham, Mama. He has already told me he does not like helping people," Eleanor broke in anxiously.

Lord Markham, who had been automatically considering how best to refuse Mrs. Needwood's importunate request, found himself exceedingly annoyed by this remark after he had done his best for Eleanor. Before he could stop himself, and just so as to wipe the smug expression off her face, he heard himself saying, "How would it be, ma'am, if I wrote to my sister? See what can be done for the girl. There's no one she doesn't know, and if she takes an interest, well, I shouldn't be surprised if she even gets vouchers for Almack's."

Mrs. Needwood was ecstatic, Miss Needwood amazed. As for Lord Markham, he was most sincerely annoyed with himself for having been lured by a wicked tongue into a situation that threatened to cost him so much effort.

CHAPTER

3

Mrs. Needwood was far too astute to ignore such an opportunity, and in the days between their meeting and the time fixed for Eleanor to go to town, many a billet-doux and brace of gamebird covered the distance between her husband's modest country estate and Lord Markham's lodge, to remind him of his obligation. Having once made up her mind to the scheme, she pursued it with a single-mindedness that typified her. It had been that and a certain ruthlessness which, a year earlier, had enabled her to entrap the gentle Mr. Needwood, so patently in a social sphere above her own, into marrying her, and, now that she had discovered his fortune (her reason for doing so!) to be less than rumor had hinted, it would be that, too, which would prevent such a trifling error from impeding her ambitions.

Thus, almost as soon as she had left Arno Grange and returned home (having first sent Sir Maltby a placatory note), she set about transforming Eleanor into *an article* fine enough to take the town by storm. By the time the viscount's sister, Lady Cecily Fienne, received the promised letter asking her to take Eleanor under her wing, the girl was a considerably altered creature from the one Lord Markham had met in Derbyshire: Her beauty undiminished, she was now a picture of elegance. Mrs. Needwood knew the value of a smart costume and spared no expense in fitting her out in the best that local modistes could offer. They had studied every recent copy of *The Ladies Magazine* they could get their hands on, had Eleanor's hair cut in a style taken from its pages, and paid attention to all those little details largely unnecessary to attract a beau in the provinces but without which no young lady in town could hope to make her way.

It was late February before Lord Markham was finally prevailed upon to write the required note to his sister. Lady Cecily received it in her dining room as she was in the process of supervising the removal of a large painting of the Battle of Edge Hill, the sale of which was necessary owing to a temporary shortage of funds.

Charmingly swathed in a voluminous old smock that only imperfectly hid her fashionable Italian dress, she was, at the moment her butler brought in her letter, standing perched on a chair directing operations. Mr. Hartley Fienne was looking on, depressed but resigned, as with her usual lack of concern his wife explained to him that with just a little retrenchment, their finances would soon be comfortable enough to buy the picture back again.

Her husband reached up his arms to her and she allowed herself to slide down into them, where he held her to him with obvious relish.

"An admirable scheme, my pet. But just when do you expect this mythical state of affairs, this agreeable plethora of money you speak of, to come about?"

"Oh, I daresay we shall soon have things easy now that I am economizing."

"Economizing, love?" he said, lifting her hand and gently nibbling her thumb. "But didn't I see Harrop taking some parcels upstairs only a few minutes ago? I think I have not forgot how parcels from Mrs. Bell are wrapped."

"Oh, but, dearest, how could I go to a rout at Melbourne House in a dress I've worn before? Sally Jersey is bound to be there, and would be sure to say something odious, which I could not bear! And in any case, it is the most charming gown. Made up in eau-de-nil taffeta, too, and only remember the other night, how much you said you'd like to see me in eau de nil."

Remembering only too well the amorous circumstances under which she had persuaded him to make such a rash statement, he pulled her closer to him, ignoring the servants, who studiously looked at the wall, while he whispered, "Fancy bringing that up in front of the servants, you witch. I swear you've no shame!"

"Very little, my love," she admitted, pouting at him entrancingly. "But you did say you liked that green."

"I accept the taffeta, but that doesn't explain the dozen or so *other* parcels."

"Oh, they were just trifles," she said airily. "Nothing to concern yourself with."

Knowing just how expensive her trifles could be, he attempted to remonstrate with her, much to her disgust.

"How unkind of you to scold me, Hart, when you know that we are living on the very edge of penury and quite without the least degree of elegance."

"Hardly that, darling. Even you can't call Grosvenor Square inelegant, and while I admit that the three or four omissions around the walls make it look a little depopulated, there's not much else we do without."

"Well, I like that! And after all my efforts. What about the little salon? I suppose you will say that I have not economized there?"

"The little salon?"

"Oh, really, Hart, don't be so provoking! I wonder why I bother sometimes. You know full well how I compromised on the new coverings for the chairs by buying that horrid straw-colored, ribbed silk!"

"But sweetheart, you had them recovered again the following week!"

"Well, of course I did. If you remember, Sally Jersey said the chairs looked like overfed canaries. You surely could not expect me to keep them after that? And it goes to prove, doesn't it, that Mama is right when she advocates always buying the very best. for no one can possibly take exception to the new peacock brocade."

"Your mama did not marry a penniless younger son," her husband reminded her.

"Not *penniless*, Hart. I won't have you put yourself down so. If your fortune is not so large as we need, it would make absolutely no difference if only Papa had not tied up my dowry until I am twenty-five."

Hartley coughed and lifted an eyebrow discreetly in the direction of the servants, who were still pretending to be blind and deaf. It was then that Lady Cecily remembered that she had not yet opened her letter, and, with a small shrug, she began to tear at the wafer.

Hartley sat down in a chair and watched, amused, for she read in much the same style as she did everything else. Each sentence met with a new play of expression, allowing him to follow the tenor of the letter with per-

23

fect ease. Before she was much into it, he knew by her frown that part, at least, did not much please her, and he dismissed the servants, deciding that they had witnessed enough indiscretions for one day. He was only just in time, for, as they closed the doors behind them his wife blurted out indignantly, "Well, of all the—"

Provokingly, she did not explain her outburst, but went on reading, until having reread some parts of it, a speculative gleam appeared in her eye.

"You may as well tell the servants to replace that painting, Hart. We won't need to sell it."

As she spoke, she handed him the letter, which he, too, quickly perused, not immediately understanding its significance with regard to the painting.

"Surely it is obvious, my love," she pointed out reasonably. "Markham wants a favor from me, and will be only too happy to settle some of our debts in return. It is perfect timing, for only think how much you'll like not having to sell old *Edge Hill*!"

"Your brother has paid quite enough of our bills."

"Why shouldn't he? He has more money than he knows what to do with. And he *likes* helping us."

It was futile to protest, for it was a plain fact that Lord Markham was more than happy to discharge their debts for them when Hartley could be prevailed upon to allow his wife to mention them. His fortune was large and, like his sister, he could see no valid reason why they should have to scrimp and save when he might assist them. As far as Lady Cecily was concerned, the matter deserved not a moment's further consideration, and they turned their attention instead back to the letter, Lady Cecily plumping herself down in her husband's lap so that she could work her way again in comfort through her brother's appalling scrawl.

"He calls Miss Needwood *unusual*, and says that he will be *happy to meet any extra costs that such a favor would incur.* And to pay any debts I find I have at present, which is dangling the carrot if ever I heard it."

"Dangling the carrot! I think it handsome."

"That's because you are a man, dearest. Men never appreciate the finer points. Very well for Markham to ask me to take the girl on, but he hasn't said *who* the Needwoods are."

"There's a Needwood family in the Midlands," he said helpfully. "Not rich, but perfectly respectable people. The girl's probably a connection. Shouldn't think Markham would send you anyone vulgar. Well, stands to reason. He doesn't know anyone but top drawer."

"Ha! That's all you know. All sorts of people turn up at *Arno*, and even in St. James's Square. And if some havey-cavey creature *has* managed to wheedle her way into his circle, it would be just like him to try to foist her off onto me. Well, I won't have it!"

"Hold on a minute, Cecy. You were just now crowing about Markham getting us out of dun territory yet again. You can't have it both ways."

"I don't mean to have it both ways. If the girl's half-way passable, naturally I would wish to oblige Markham, for you know how I dote on him. But only imagine if she's a fright! I could not do it, even for my brother. Only think how lowering it would be to have the patronesses at Almack's refuse one a voucher! Sally Jersey would love nothing more. Why, Mama would never forgive me. To be on the safe side, I think it only fair to make my position known to Markham from the start. If the girl's an upstart, *nothing* will induce me to take her on. I shall write and tell him so."

As a result of these sisterly heart-searchings, the following missive, in Lady Cecily's flowing hand, arrived on the viscount's breakfast table two days later. "My dearest Markham," it began.

How perfectly splendid to have your letter after so long (for I declare you have not replied to any of mine for months). And what are you doing at *Arno*? I had quite expected you in town by now. Half London seems to have returned early, and the season is already the most unbearable squeeze, which you will not like to miss. If I did not know how indolent you are, I'd swear you were keeping a fair Paphian at the lodge and shocking your neighbors.

Now! Let us speak of your plans for the unusual Miss Needwood. How sublime of you to promise the girl's mama that I shall take her in hand. And what a mind reader you must be to be able to do so without asking me first. Wicked Markham! Dearest, I really cannot allow you to decide in whom I shall take an interest, for if the girl is a City mushroom (or worse!) nothing could persuade me. Not even if you promised me a new court dress like the delightful one I saw at Mrs. Bell's establishment the other day! (Hart says I must not write that last sentence, so pray consider it crossed through, if you please.)

On the other hand, sweet, dear Markham, if I find her partway to being a lady, well—we shall see!

I note that you say that you wish to do the girl a
26

good turn. How is it that your good turns always entail other people bestirring themselves?

Fondest love,
Cecy

P.S. Hart asks if he should put me on a diet of bread and water for my incivility.

CHAPTER

4

Mrs. Needwood explained to her husband that it would be foolishly expensive to take the younger girls to London for Eleanor's come-out, and elected instead to leave them in the country with their new papa. It remained for her only to obtain a new governess to take Eleanor's place in the schoolroom and hire a post chaise to take them to town.

Before they left, Eleanor went to say good-bye to her father and found him in his succession houses, where he usually escaped from his wife. He started guiltily when her shadow fell on him as he lazed on a bench seat in the early morning sunshine.

"It's all right, Papa, it's only me. Mama is still directing the servants," Eleanor assured him with a hug.

He shifted uncomfortably.

"I'm not afraid of your mama, Nell," he said firmly, sounding so much like Papa of old that she felt a strong upsurge of nostalgia for their old, easy life, before Stepmama's rule had changed everything.

"I'm sorry, Papa. I didn't mean anything. And at least my London season will give you some peace from Stepmama's nagging. I only hope you will be able to manage things on the estate without me, for you know how you hate dealing with domestic quarrels when they arise."

"I can bear domestic quarrels on the estate far more than at home, Nell. But I wish you would not speak so disparagingly of your stepmama," he said, covering her hand with his own. "People don't like to hear young girls speak ill of their parents, no matter that they deserve it. Try, if you can, not to let this marriage of mine sour you. Take it instead as a warning to look around you carefully for a suitable husband. Remember how happy your own dear mama made me. Don't ever forget, my love, how important it is to marry someone harmonious to your spirit."

"Yet you would have let Stepmama marry me off to Sir Maltby."

He rubbed his forefinger back and forth across his forehead. "I like to think that I'd have found the strength to intervene, Nell, my darling. And maybe, in memory of your own dear mama, I would have. In any case, that's neither here nor there, for your stepmama wants bigger fish now. But remember, sweeting, how your mama can be swayed by, well, by more venal considerations—though she means it only for the best. Try to be firm, if you can, and not let yourself be persuaded into a match you cannot like, just because a man is wealthy. And remember, too, that you are sometimes a thought too high-spirited for your own good, so don't get into any scrapes. I wish I had some suitable female in the family I could send you to, m'dear, but the only person I still keep in touch with is old Colonel Aspley. He lives too far from the thick of things to be of any use to you, I'm afraid."

"Don't worry about me, Papa," she said, kissing him

on both cheeks. "Now that Lord Markham has persuaded Mama, I don't mean to make a mull of it. There must be a young man somewhere who will suit us both!"

Mrs. Needwood had hired a charming little house in Keppel Street. Never having had a season herself, she saw no reason why she should not enjoy Eleanor's; indeed, she spent rather more on her own wardrobe than her stepdaughter's, excusing herself on the grounds that if her daughter were to be properly launched, it would never do for her family to appear shabby ("However much trouble it has caused poor Mama!"). Eleanor's gowns must be elegant but simple, as befitted a young woman making her debut: Her own had to be something more, for she could not bear to shame the darling girl!

Far too shrewd to force the pace, they made a quiet entrance to the London season. Rushing matters never answered, and she insisted that they feel their way for several weeks before she judged it time to leave her visiting card with the Lady Cecily.

Mrs. Needwood had been surprised to find how many invitations to ton parties they had received meanwhile, not knowing that she had her husband to thank for it. Eleanor's papa was not wealthy (the only yardstick *she* knew by which to measure standing), but his connections were impeccable, and many a matronly society lady remembered having her heart dented by dashing young Mr. Needwood, as he had been a quarter of a century earlier.

For his sake they welcomed his wife and daughter, and the girl held her breath, wondering how soon it would be before they were disgusted by Mrs. Needwood's encroaching ways. But she had underestimated

Stepmama. Quick to learn, Mrs. Needwood soon altered her public manner to match theirs, so that the forwardness that had them stiffening up receded almost at once, leaving them to wonder if they had not imagined it. Eleanor could only be amused by Mama's cleverness, but she was relieved not to have to feel shame for her. With her relief came a new public respect, and they had passed easily into fashionable circles by the time they left their card with Lady Cecily's butler.

It was a gratifying surprise when at their first at-home morning afterward, Mrs. Needwood's butler brought in on a salver Lady Cecily's gold-edged visiting card, and she went forward to greet her visitor with swelling bosom, delighted to see her so soon.

Lady Cecily entered Mrs. Needwood's salon in a flurry of ivory bombazine and sables, her hand outstretched to greet her hostess and a tentative smile on her lips. The smile deepened on noting Mrs. Needwood's smart *percale* half-dress and Eleanor's clear lawn, for she would clearly have no need to blush for the way either lady dressed.

Mrs. Needwood's overfulsome welcome she could not admire, but her brother's letter had hinted that the girl was more worth knowing then the mother. Having ensured that the older lady was not *so* vulgar as to make the connection ineligible, she turned her attention to Eleanor, who was quite overawed by the tall, smart society lady facing her. She had somehow expected her to be more homely.

Remembering how her stepmama had shamefully manipulated their introduction, she was sure Lady Cecily must expect the worst. Her anxious eyes and worried little frown did her no disservice with Lady

Cecily, who had an overwhelming urge to put her at her ease.

"How fortunate that we are both of us tall," she observed with satisfaction. "It would have been too provoking going about together had we not been much of a height, whatever Markham wished."

"What an awkward situation your brother has placed you in, ma'am. Please say if it will not suit you to give me your protection. I am sure that it must be a good deal of trouble."

"Well, it must, of course," Cecily said candidly. "For I have promised Markham to get you vouchers for Almack's, and Lady Jersey will certainly try to deny them, for she and I are always at odds. Indeed, I am not at all fond of her, with her tragical airs, though one must not say so, naturally. But I *shall* get you vouchers. Emily Cowper has a passion for Markham, and if she should fail me, which I by no means expect, I can always ask Lady Sefton, for she is too indolent to refuse."

Eleanor blinked at the catalogue of illustrious names, feeling quite crushed. "How dreadful to put you out so. Your brother cannot have realized what he was asking."

Seeing the faint blush that had spread over Eleanor's cheeks when she mentioned Lord Markham, and entirely mistaking her embarrassment for a different emotion, Lady Cecily felt a twinge of suspicion, which the girl's beauty strongly reinforced. She returned to Grosvenor Square later that morning, her mind working busily. Swinging her bonnet by its ribbons, the ostrich plumes that had cost a guinea each from Mr. Botibol's shop only the week before dangling on the floor, she dashed into her husband's study, where she found him dictating letters. Recognizing her "at-once" expression, he dismissed his secretary, wondering what mischief she was up to now.

As soon as they were alone, she burst out with "What would you say if I told you Markham was in love?"

"I'd say it was all a hum," he said, and he turned back to the papers on his desk.

Lady Cecily pouted, and marched away in a huff, to stare out at the circular park below. Coming up and embracing her from behind a few moments later, her husband brushed his cheek against her hair.

"All right, jade, you win. What makes you think that Markham is in love?"

Her temper evaporated at once in her impatience to share with him her suspicions, and she turned in his arms to catch at the collar of his coat. "It is so *obvious*, Hart, that it is a wonder I didn't see it before," she cried. "Time and again you've said that you wonder that Markham should ask me to put myself out for a provincial nobody, haven't you?"

"Actually, love, it was *you* who said she was a provincial nobody. I said that she probably belonged to that Midland family, if you—"

"Oh, do stop interrupting, Hart! We were *both* surprised. You know we were. That Markham even bothered to write should have alerted us! But now it is quite clear why he should try to smooth things for her."

"You've seen Miss Needwood, I collect? And she's obviously no antidote, or you wouldn't be hopping up and down on one foot. But that's not enough to have you ordering the orange blossom. If he intended to marry Miss Needwood, they'd be in town together."

"Oh, you know Markham." She shrugged. "The season's still sluggish. He never comes to town until it's a crush."

"Doing it rather too brown, Cecy, my love. Even your precious brother wouldn't remain at Arno if the object of his affections was in London."

"I'll lay you a pony I'm right," she said with decision.

"Lay me a pony! My dear girl, where do you think you could lay your hands on twenty pounds at this moment? And where *do* you pick up these expressions?"

"From you, of course, and I shall keep you to it, so have your money ready. As for me, I'd better get on with securing vouchers for Almack's at once. Not that it will be difficult now, for I have only to whisper that Miss Needwood is Markham's inamorata. Even Lady Jersey would not refuse vouchers to the wife of the future Earl of Fildes!"

"Cecy! What if you're wrong!"

"But I don't *mean* to be wrong, Hart, darling."

"Cecy," said her husband, suddenly suspicious. "You *want* something from all this."

"I?" she cried, looking the picture of innocence. "You are the greatest brute in the world to say so. But Markham has to be married sometime, my love," she continued with charming inconsistency.

"Markham married? I never saw anyone so set against it."

"Hush—I'm talking. Now, who is he likely to fall back on if he doesn't marry Miss Needwood? Miss Tantrell or Miss Bourne-Setham, for you'll never get me to admit that Miss Smyth stands the vaguest chance."

"I don't think he likes any of them."

34

"But he'll marry one of 'em, for he's nearly thirty, and Papa keeps going on at him. And if he does so, how will that help us?"

"Does he know that is to be his first consideration?"

She ignored him. "If, on the other hand, he marries Miss Needwood—well!" she said, as if all should now be blindingly clear.

"Well—what?"

"Oh, really, Hart, keep up! If I bring Miss Needwood into fashion, it'll be all but impossible for her to stop Markham helping us out financially when they are married. Any of the others would be sure to nag him about it. Miss Needwood will understand that she owes me a debt. And even if her gratitude wears off after a while, which it is bound to do, no matter, for I get my own fortune in two years. It'll tide us over nicely until then."

"So you don't really think that Markham is in love with Miss Needwood at all?" said Hartley with a confused look. "Then you can't possibly spread rumors about them. Think how embarrassing it would be for them."

"Very likely he is in love with her, Hart. Why would he have written else? And it's no wonder, for she's charming and beautiful, with the drollest sense of humor. Of course he has fallen in love."

CHAPTER

5

Having decided that Miss Needwood was to be her brother's intended, Lady Cecily spared no pains to ingratiate the girl into her own set. It was soon an accustomed thing to see them out shopping in Bond Street, changing books at Hatcham's, and arriving together at receptions.

Dropping just a *hint* of her suspicions in Lady Cowper's ear, Almack's vouchers were promptly supplied, and before Eleanor had danced more than two nights away there, the whole town discussed the rumor of a betrothal. Now everyone wanted to know Eleanor, and Mrs. Needwood preened herself at their good fortune without understanding it. Lord Markham's absence from town caused hardly a ripple, for he was a byword for laziness, disliked society, and stayed away from town as often as he could. It was amusing but not entirely out of character that he remained in Derbyshire, leaving the beautiful girl they had promoted to his betrothed to fend for herself. Miss Needwood's lack of fortune was mentioned as a barrier to the match, but few believed that a girl Markham was after really had no fortune, and even such mar-joys who did soon acknowledged that fortune was unnecessary in a wife when one was as rich as he.

Only an impeccable lineage was needed, and that Eleanor had.

Having disposed of this delicate matter, all seemed set for a triumph—until disaster came in a letter from Mr. Needwood of such moment that his wife was obliged to post home at once!

It was unfortunate, but there was nothing to be done. Having been in London a month, Eleanor called on Lady Cecily to take her leave.

Seeing Eleanor's puffy eyes, she rushed the visitors to her boudoir. "What has happened, my love?" she asked when they were alone. "You've been crying!"

Before Eleanor had a chance to say so much as a word, her stepmama burst into tears.

"My dear Lady Cecily, we are undone!" she sobbed, dabbing her eyes with her handkerchief. "We have had word from Eleanor's papa that my daughter Charlotte has the whooping cough. Eleanor's papa absolutely insists that I return to Derbyshire at once, though what he expects me to do for Charlotte that would not be done by her governess, I cannot imagine."

"But you will surely *wish* to nurse your child yourself?" said Lady Cecily in some surprise.

"If I had only my own wishes to consult, I should be already on my way home," Mrs. Needwood unhesitatingly perjured herself. "But Eleanor's future, too, is in my hands. I count *that* a solemn trust, as you may imagine." She paused, wondering if she had gone too far, but seeing only sympathy on Lady Cecily's face did not hesitate to lay it on with a trowel, and thickly. "And if I have to go home, Eleanor must go, too. Just when everything was going so well. The house in Keppel Street must be closed down, and indeed, should I be detained long in Derbyshire, it seems hardly worth keeping it on at all, such an expense as it is. The season will be all but gone by the time Charlotte can be expected to be well."

Lady Cecily—to whom this aspect of the case had not been immediately apparent—bit her lip, as much vexed as Mrs. Needwood by the thought of having to stand by and see Eleanor abandon London so soon. *She* didn't wish it, and she persuaded herself, too, that it was not at all what her brother would wish, either. She cast about for a way to keep her in town.

A solution presented itself at once. Why should not Eleanor stay with *her* in Grosvenor Square? Markham would certainly expect it, and it would in any case be delightful. Mrs. Needwood, too, liked the idea, for it was difficult to conceive of a way of continuing Eleanor's debut at so little cost to herself. And perhaps, when tiresome little Charlotte could be encouraged to admit herself recovered, Mrs. Needwood might even be able to take advantage herself of the surprising spaciousness of the Grosvenor Square mansion!

Eleanor was in a quandary, convinced that her duty lay at home nursing Charlotte, for she knew how nervous the little girl was of Mama. Mrs. Needwood would not hear of it. Taking Eleanor aside, she read her a lecture on the virtues of obedience, reminded her of her own considerable efforts on her behalf, and clinched the matter by recalling Sir Maltby's proposal. Eleanor might not even then have capitulated, but remembered in time her stepmama's reluctance to enter a sickroom, and the certainty that Charlotte's new governess would be called upon to nurse the sick child. Mrs. Needwood posted home that very day, leaving behind her only a proviso forbidding Cecily to arrange for Eleanor's presentation at court until she returned—for she had no intention of missing that! Within the day Eleanor had moved into a pretty little blue-and-white bedroom on the second floor at Lady Cecily's.

Letters from Mama were awaited fearfully at first, on account of Charlotte (though they appeared chiefly to bemoan the child's willfulness in insisting on continuing with "the whoop" at such a time), and Eleanor was ready to go home at a moment's notice if her sister appeared to need her. Her father's early P.S. quickly reassured them: Though "still very poorly," Charlotte was now rather better than she had been, and the new governess was "not only a favorite already with the child, but a sensible woman, perfectly fit to take charge of the sickroom." Her mind at peace, Eleanor persuaded herself to be led by the Lady Cecily into a season of enjoyment.

Once it was known that Eleanor was residing with Lady Cecily, most of those who had held out against a romance with Lord Markham were silenced. Mountains of invitation cards arrived, and it seemed to Eleanor that from the moment they arose until they lay down exhausted heads in the early hours, they all rushed insanely from one social event to another. Rout balls followed alfresco expeditions to Kew and other gardens; masquerade balls nudged on to receptions and parties so that when Eleanor had been only a few weeks in town, she was able to remark, with a perfect assumption of fashionable ennui, what a bore it all was.

And all the time, without any encouragement from the two principals, the fascinating rumor of Eleanor's marriage to Markham continued to be a matter for delighted speculation.

Not too surprisingly, that same rumor finally circulated to the borders of Wiltshire and Somerset, more especially to Fildes Castle, the Earl of Fildes's country seat. It was to the countess that the disturbing whisper found its way, and on receiving a hint of what was being said in a letter from Lady Jersey, one of her best correspondents, along with the news that Miss Needwood was residing with Cecily, she hurried off to seek her husband. She found him in his gun room, where he had taken delivery of a hunting rifle that moment arrived from Manton's and, as she entered the room, he had just lifted it to his shoulder to get the feel of it. She started abruptly to see him pointing the weapon at her and backed toward the doorway again.

Her husband laughed. "It isn't loaded, my dear. Never fear! Did you think I was trying to do away with you?"

"Certainly! Were you not saying at breakfast that the world would be a better place if the Lord had left Adam's ribs intact?"

Grimacing, the earl laid down the gun, and then drew his wife toward him, kissing her forehead. "That's because I'm a crusty old fool. But you know by now, Maria, how I hate conversation at the breakfast table."

"Hardly conversation, dear," she reminded him with misleading humility. "I asked you if you wanted another egg, as I remember."

Laughing, he gave her a hearty squeeze. "I know it! I'm a Tartar. But at least it's only at the breakfast table. I usually cheer up by luncheon, don't I, unless something else happens to vex me."

"I'm very much afraid that something else *has*," said his wife, repeating the substance of her letter and waiting for the explosion to follow.

The earl was used to ruling the roost, and by the completion of Lady Fildes's recital, his habitually ruddy cheeks had deepened three shades. He spluttered to find his words and finally let out a bellow of rage. "That boy! How *dare* he become betrothed without telling me first! And him here not more than ten days since, without saying a word! What price filial devotion, my lady, heh? M'father would have had me horsewhipped if I'd done such a ramshackle thing!"

"Hardly *boy*, dearest, and the letter mentions only the *rumor* of an attachment," she said soothingly. "Sally Jersey may have it wrong—probably has, indeed, for the girl has been staying with Cecily for the past two weeks and Cecily has written nothing about an attachment in *her* letters."

"I've never known Sally Jersey to get the wrong end of any gossip, Maria. Something must have occurred to make her whiskers twitch. And everyone in on it but his own parents! I give you leave to consider what sort of a fool that makes *me* look!"

"You are being too harsh on Markham," she said gently. "Perhaps that was his purpose in coming to see us, dearest. And then you argued again. How could he tell you after that?"

"So! It's *my* fault! You always take his part against me."

"Only when you are being unfair."

"Which is always, according to you."

She smiled. "Not quite always. Sometimes, just sometimes when you are dealing with that precious son

41

of ours, you are quite human. But I do happen to think it *was* your fault last time. You shouldn't have nagged him about the north barn at Arno. It's his own property, and he can do as he wishes with it."

"But that's just the point! He doesn't do *anything* with it! Whole place is tumbling down. Bates wrote to me about it weeks ago. Said the whole roof will fall through if he doesn't see to it."

"And you couldn't bear not to tell him of it, dear, could you, though you know how he hates Bates reporting such things to you. He says Bates spies on him. You always handle him so badly. I am sure that he would do more at Arno if you didn't try to nag him into it. And, incidentally, if you didn't encourage Bates to tell you about every blade of grass on the property."

"Bates sees things just as he ought. He's a sensible man. If Markham didn't have Bates, the whole estate would be a cabbage patch by now! Imagine Gawaine letting his lands go the way Markham has let go the Arno estate."

"Gawaine is in the navy, dearest, because he doesn't have any lands to let go but the little estate at Fradingham," she pointed out. "And you have been looking after that for him."

"Never mind that! It's Markham we're talking about. And he shows no sense at all when it comes to property."

"If you must know, Markham told *me* that before you and Bates started to interfere, he had every intention of rebuilding the north barn. Besides, whose fault is it if Markham has no farming sense? Whenever he has tried to interest himself in the estates at Fildes, you have as good as told him to mind his own business."

"He's perfectly free to do what he likes at Arno, if he ever does *anything* with it! Time enough for him to ruin this place when it's his!" he said with what sounded to him like perfect sense. "But there! I knew it would all come back to me. It always does. And I suppose it is I who taught him to kick his heels in Derbyshire like a nodcock while the girl he hopes to marry is in town! I can just imagine what they are making of that in the clubs."

His wife smiled a knowing little smile. "No, I don't think even I can say he has inherited his patience in love from you. He is past even my defending in that. Not a patch on his father. You didn't give me a moment's peace once you'd decided to marry *me*."

Reluctantly he grinned, which had the happy effect of making his ruddy countenance look quite boyish. "Dash it all, Maria, no man would have been able to stay away from *you*. Not me, anyway. I couldn't do it then, and I've never been able to do it since."

"I should hope not!" She laughed, pinching his chin. "But do you not find it strange that he should not be in town at such a time—if the rumors are true? And this girl, dearest. I wonder what she's like."

"It makes no difference what she's like," said the earl, picking up the rifle and fitting it into a case on the wall. "Markham can't throw himself away on a provincial nobody. Girl's got no fortune. Says so in that letter. My heir can have his pick of the best of 'em."

"You threw yourself away on a provincial nobody, as I remember," she reminded him.

He flushed a deep red and said gruffly, "You were never that, Maria. Had the town at your feet."

43

"From what Sally Jersey says, so has Miss Needwood, and she's better connected that I was."

The earl stopped dead in his tracks. "Do I understand that you mean to encourage Markham in his madness? I know you dote on the boy, but surely . . ."

"I do not *dote* on him, as you so foolishly put it, but I do want him to be happy. He'll be thirty next birthday, and I for one would like some grandchildren before I'm too crotchety to enjoy them. And I don't want to see him trapped by someone like that Lady Violet Pelham, who had her hooks into him last year. Nor do I want him going through a marriage of convenience to get an heir. At least he apparently likes this girl, and she does have a decent background."

"Good God, Maria, you've set your heart on this, haven't you?" replied her husband. "I can't believe it."

"I want to see him married, darling. It would make me very happy."

"Then I suppose we had better go to see Cecy and look the girl over."

The countess reminded him that since Lord Markham was still in Derbyshire, the affair could not as yet have been brought to a conclusion, and she cautioned him against interfering. He pooh-poohed the matter in his usual high-handed manner, defended his right to pay his married daughter a visit, and ordered their baggage to be made ready for the following day.

44

CHAPTER

6

It was Hartley who went out to meet their carriage when the earl and his wife arrived in Grosvenor Square two days later, for Cecily felt ill with apprehension. The rumor that she had taken such pains to circulate must have reached home! Mama, at least, would require to know why she had not learned of it from her daughter. Now, Cecily certainly had every intention of continuing with her plan (when Markham eventually showed himself in town), but she had fondly imagined that before Mama and Papa were brought into the picture, Markham might have been firmly secured. The situation required careful handling. Assuming her most artless expression, she hurried to meet her parents.

Eleanor remained out of the way in a corner with her tambour frame, from where she was at liberty to take stock of the arrivals. The earl was quite a disappointment to her. She had formed a mental picture of him that this stocky, red-faced man, dressed in a perfectly ordinary drab greatcoat and low beaver could hardly be said to tally. Her vision had taught her to expect a tall, slender Adonis, sometimes in magnificent evening dress, sometimes (in her more fanciful moods) in robes, but never in exactly the same style of raiment as her own father might have worn! She smiled to herself at her foolishness just as the countess chanced to look over at her. Thus Lord Markham's mama was privileged to see at its best the face about which all London was talking. And if her son had fallen in love with such a face, who could blame him? She went over at once to be introduced to the girl whom she one day expected to be calling daughter.

Eager to put her at her ease, the countess engaged Eleanor in conversation, determined to discover what had taken her son's fancy, for she doubted that Markham would be captured by only a pretty face. It was too much to expect the earl to allow his wife to monopolize Miss Needwood when he had come so many miles to see her for himself. Flicking up his coat-tails and warming himself at the fireplace, he interrupted his wife in full flow.

"Well, now, Miss Needwood," he said brightly with a determinedly cheerful expression. "Tell us all about yourself. Father. Mother—that sort of thing!"

"You will have to excuse Fildes, Miss Needwood," interpolated Lady Fildes, glaring at her husband. "Really, I *have* tried to instill in him some of the social graces, but as you can see, it is uphill work."

Her husband stared back seraphically. "What have I said now?"

"And the best of it is, my dear," Lady Fildes explained to Eleanor, "that he really *doesn't* know! It is an accepted thing in company, Fildes, that one engage in conversation. If you want to *interrogate* somebody, go and join the army!"

"I *am* engaging in conversation, Maria!"

"Then try and do it properly. Don't bark at Miss Needwood, or you will scare her away."

"Miss Needwood won't mind me, will you, missie? I'm a plain man. Old-fashioned. Believe in plain dealing, and that's a fact. Tell me about your family, girl. Who's your father? Do I *know* him?"

"Miss Needwood's father has an estate in Derbyshire, Papa," Cecily hastened to explain, eager for Eleanor to appear in the best possible light.

"Miss Needwood can answer for herself, can't she?"

"Indeed I can," Eleanor agreed as Cecily docilely sank back against the cushions. "Papa is Mr. Henry Needwood, sir, of Evendale in Derbyshire," she explained as succinctly as even the earl could require, "but I shouldn't think you will have known him, for he was in London for only a season, as I understand it, and that was more than twenty years ago. Besides, he will have been quite beneath your touch!"

"But not mine, I fancy, Miss Needwood," said Lady Fildes kindly, favorably impressed by the girl's refusal to prevaricate. "My own family, too, are well beneath my husband's touch. There was a merry dance when he wanted to marry me."

Certain that her scolding must encourage her husband toward more proper behavior, the countess had reckoned without the earl who, glaring at his wife from the corner of his eye, asked Eleanor carelessly, "Large property is it, this Evendale?"

Lady Fildes raised horrified eyes. "You see what I'm up against, my dear. Really, I can accept no responsibility for him."

"Oh, tosh, Maria."

The earl and the countess stayed in town for a week,

47

during which time Lady Fildes had ample time to satisfy herself that Eleanor would do for her son. In that unusually benevolent lady's eyes, the amassing of family fortunes had always held a low place. Her own had been a love match, and she could not bear to think that any of her children should be forced to settle for anything less. She had once read in *Poor Richard's Alamanac*, Benjamin Franklin's famous line, that "where there's marriage without love there will be love without marriage," and had never forgotten it. She found the earliest opportunity for a tête-à-tête with her daughter to get the facts, and was frankly disappointed to hear that nothing was really *settled* at all between her son and Miss Needwood.

But when Cecily, building it up to suit herself, told how Lord Markham had met Eleanor first in Derbyshire and had then pressed his sister to sponsor her (managing magnificently to imply that Markham's exertions on the girl's behalf, far from consisting of rather more than six lines in a letter, resembled the labors of Hercules), Lady Fildes sat looking very thoughtful indeed. The more she thought about it, the more it seemed that Markham *must* be in love, as Lady Jersey had hinted. Sally Jersey might be a trifle quick off the mark with her talk of wedding banns, but certainly Markham had an interest.

She determined to get to know Eleanor properly, and finding herself alone with her one morning, fell into amiable conversation. She soon had from her a description of her first meeting with Markham, which soon had her giggling like a schoolgirl, and being Eleanor, her tongue ran on about how she had nagged him about his way of running his estates.

48

So that is how he came to fall in love, thought Lady Fildes in amusement. *Markham was piqued by her criticism!* But when she had leisure to reflect on their conversation later, Lady Fildes could not help but admit that Eleanor had said no more about her son than did his own father. It *was* bad husbandry to leave Arno to fend for itself, just as Fildes always complained. She became sunk in deep thought, wondering if Eleanor's criticism meant that she could not care for her son. What a pity that would be, for the more she got to know her, the more she became convinced that Miss Needwood might be just right for him. If Eleanor could only get him to put his house in order, how much more harmonious life might be. A rosy image of filial visits, enhanced by Markham's pretty wife (and perhaps even one or two babies), filled the countess's vision. She had come up to town prepared to be pleased with Miss Needwood, but now, when she looked again at the girl, she saw not only the beautiful face and pretty manner that must have captivated her son, but an air of decision that would be the very best thing in the world in his wife. Certainly *she* would put nothing in the way were such a marriage mooted.

Having made up her own mind, it was only a matter of time before she had convinced her husband not just that he agreed, but that the notion had been his own all along. He wanted to write to his son at once, but his wife convinced him that Markham must be allowed to make his move in his own time.

By the time Lord and Lady Fildes had been in town a few days, Eleanor was being treated like one of their family. She was soon being called by her first name, and the earl had even danced twice with her at

Almack's! Cecily's parents liked the girl, and they returned to Somerset a week later, eager to hear that the match was made.

Eleanor could not help remarking how she would miss them.

"I cannot imagine why they should have treated me so kindly," she said as they came away from the windows at which they had been waving.

Without thinking Cecily replied, "Well, of course they did, Nell, dearest. Now that they know you're to *marry* my brother, they want you to *feel* like a daughter."

Eleanor stared incredulously. "Marry your brother?"

The startled look on her friend's face caused Cecily to swallow hard. "Well, yes, Nell. You *are* going to marry Markham, aren't you? Everyone thinks you are!"

"Why on earth should anyone think I am going to marry Lord Markham? I've met him only once! You surely did not think it, did you, Cecy?"

"I *did*, actually," Cecily replied somewhat haughtily, seeing her precious plan falling about her. "When he wrote to me about you, you know."

"But that's mad! You've never said so much as a word about such a thing! Why didn't you ask me if you thought that?"

"I thought you must want to keep it a secret until Markham came to town," she said sulkily, unwilling to admit even to herself that she had fabricated the whole thing.

"But that's ridiculous! And you say *everyone* thinks it! But how can that be?"

"I expect it is because I have been sponsoring you, Nell, dear. Your staying here, too. You know how people catch hold of quaint ideas. And, indeed, I suppose it is really no wonder that they should, for Markham never puts himself out for anyone, and to ask me to take you under my wing was so unlike!"

"Oh, Cecy! So that is why you asked me to stay here! I feel so awful! I must leave at once!"

She had a sudden fleeting thought and put her hands to her cheeks, which were suddenly pink. "Oh, and, Cecy, please do write to your mama tomorrow and explain matters! How dreadful that she should think such a thing of me. Why, she even spoke to me about Markham! Oh, I wish I could remember what I said about him! She must think I'm a *fortune* hunter."

"Stuff and nonsense, Nell. She thinks no such thing. She likes you! She would *love* to see you marry Markham."

"That's absurd. Your brother might marry anyone, I daresay."

"Mama does not care for such things."

"But I do! I don't want to marry Lord Markham. I don't even *know* him. You must write to Lady Fildes at once."

This, however, Cecily had absolutely no intention of doing. Even if she was forced to admit that Markham had no interest in Eleanor after all, it didn't mean he *wouldn't* have! He *had* asked her to sponsor Eleanor, so he *must* like her! And when Markham came to town Cecily would see to it that she threw them together all the time! She might yet bring it off! And it would be so *convenient* having Nell as a sister! She took Eleanor in her arms and hugged her.

"Well, you're not leaving here, anyway," she said briskly. "I can't do without you, so that's settled! And you are not to tell *anyone* that we have had this little bit of confusion about Markham."

"I should love to stay, Cecy, but I don't see how I can. And it's silly to say that we mustn't tell people the truth!"

"It isn't so very silly when you think about it. Markham went to a good deal of trouble to persuade me to sponsor you, and all so that you would be accepted in ton circles, but if they hear that you've misled them, it will all have been for nothing. They'll ignore you. Refuse you vouchers for Almack's!" The thought made Cecily shudder. "Only think how upset Markham will be if his efforts on your behalf fail."

"I don't see that it makes that much difference," said Eleanor philosophically. "Indeed, if everyone thinks I'm going to marry Lord Markham, I wonder that anyone has shown any interest in me at all!"

"Well, they *have*. Mr. Holbrook would marry you tomorrow if you gave him any encouragement," said Cecily, naming one of Eleanor's most persistent followers. "And there are plenty of others."

"But how can I possibly make an eligible connection if I'm supposed to be already betrothed? It's impossible. I might as well go home."

"Don't be a goose, Nell. The best way of handling this affair is to say nothing. Carry on staying here, for I really do want you. And so does Hart! When Markham comes to town and no betrothal is announced, it will probably be assumed that it was all idle gossip, and the matter will be allowed to drop. And if the patronesses at Almack's become difficult, Markham will be here to wheedle vouchers from Emily Cowper. Don't worry about a thing. As soon as Markham arrives, I'll get Hart to explain it all to him!"

With this Eleanor was obliged to be content, and she waited, with some trepidation, for the arrival of her supposed suitor.

Meanwhile, having seen Eleanor appearing in public with Lord Markham's parents, the last dissenters from the polite world had been silenced. By the time the viscount arrived in town, his marriage to Miss Needwood was quite a settled thing.

CHAPTER

7

He was at Brooks's Club in St. James's Street when Markham caught up with the rumor. He had been in town only a few hours and, after changing his traveling garb for the dark blue dress coat and pantaloons for correct evening attire, made his way to his club. Ambling into the Great Subscription Room on the first floor, the first person he ran into was his brother-in-law, who had not had to accompany his wife to the weekly ball at Almack's, a piece of self-interest made possible when some admirers of his wife begged to be allowed to take her instead. The brothers-in-law had little in common, but had always rather liked each other, and it was with a touch of surprise that Lord Markham noticed a hint of reluctance in Hartley's greeting, sufficient to alert him. When the room at large noticed him, went quiet for a moment, and then disguised it by coughs and forced conversation, he was on his guard.

Hartley, as malleable in Lord Markham's hands as in Lady Cecily's, soon admitted to the rumor that had all London by the ears. Markham was at first inclined to be skeptical. Nobody but a fool could possibly be taken in by such an unfounded rumor! But when Hartley, with great presence of mind, had the betting book brought and showed him three separate bets entered there on the probable length of time it would take Lord Markham to come to the point in the small matter of his betrothal, he could hardly doubt any longer.

He was most seriously grieved.

"This comes of trying to do the girl a good turn! I should have known she'd be like her stepmama!"

Hartley could hardly sit by and hear Miss Needwood maligned so unfairly; neither was he courageous enough to inform Markham whom he really had to thank for spreading the regrettable story. "I say, old fellow, don't you think that's a bit strong?" he ventured to put forth. "Charming girl, Miss Needwood. Not an ounce of vice in her. I'd stake my reputation that it wasn't she who spread the rumors. She's not the type, and *I* know her about as well as anybody. Matter of fact, she's staying with us in Grosvenor Square."

"Staying with *you*?" Lord Markham's eyes widened in horror, then he groaned and rested his head in his hands.

It was with an enormous sense of ill usage that the viscount set out early next afternoon from his house in St. James's Square to visit his sister's home, where he intended to give Miss Needwood a piece of his mind. He took with him a throbbing head, for he had met up with some friends on the previous evening and had gone on with them to spend a convivial night at the Daffy Club in Holborn.

He turned his carriage into Green Park, hoping that he wouldn't see too many people he knew on the way to Grosvenor Square and be forced to be sociable. He was fortunate, for almost at once he ran into Hartley and the Lady Cecily taking the air with Eleanor, and was saved the trouble of seeking them out.

In truth, Markham did not immediately recognize Eleanor, and was just going to lecture his sister on the imprudence of taking fortune-grabbing harpies into one's home, when Eleanor turned on him her unforgettable eyes. Lord Markham held up his quizzing glass and stared in openmouthed appreciation at the vision in cerulean blue that stood before him.

"Good God, Miss Needwood, is that you? What a dasher you've become!"

If he was surprised at how well she looked, Eleanor was equally taken aback by him. Last time she'd seen him he had been in his shirt-sleeves, but Lord Markham in town was an altogether different species. Nothing had prepared her for this pink of the ton who sat gazing down at her, and she stared at him with frank admiration, taking in his immaculate morning coat, tight pantaloons, and shiny Hessians. She held up her hand to greet him, saying with an unaffected twinkle, "Will it sink me if I say the same to you, Lord Markham? Now if you had only rescued Mama dressed like *that*, you'd have escaped the ignominy of being thought a farm laborer."

His anger evaporated at once, and he became unaccountably quite certain that she had set no deliberate trap to entice him into marriage. He took her hand in his. "Still got that dashed pleasant tongue, I see," he returned.

"Oh, no! How infamous of you to say so when I have been quite on my best behavior."

"But your best behavior is really so much worse than everybody else's!"

"Humph! I liked you better when you were fighting my battles for me in Derbyshire."

Her mention of Derbyshire brought him back to their immediate problem, and he begged her urgently to take a turn about Green Park with him so as to broach the subject. As soon as they were enough out of earshot he asked, "Well, Miss Needwood, and how do you like London? I suppose you are like every other woman I know and would wish to stay forever?"

"I like it very well, sir," she answered with a smile. "Though I doubt I'd like to stay forever."

"Now, why am I surprised when you give me a perfectly unaccountable answer?" said Markham, holding his head on one side to look at her. "I thought you couldn't wait to get here."

"Do not mistake, sir," she said kindly. "Indeed I *am* grateful to be here. It's just . . ."

"Don't spare my feelings, Miss Needwood."

"It's only that I find it so extraordinary that nobody I meet ever seems to do anything *useful*! It appears to be one long round of pleasure from dawn to dusk."

"Is that so very dreadful?" he asked, taken aback.

"Not too very dreadful, perhaps, but does it seem quite right? I confess that when I go to church on Sunday I sometimes wonder if—"

"This seems to be where we began," said Markham, looking faintly amused. "I should love to hear you asking my sister if she shouldn't be occupying herself usefully."

"I *did* ask Cecy something of the sort when I first came to stay," Eleanor confessed. "I thought I might help her, naturally. But when I asked on what day of the week we should do our sewing for the indigent, she said

57

that one didn't do that sort of thing in the season, which seems quite odd. One has only to look about to see that there are vast numbers of needy—"

"And how did she take this dressing-down, my sister?"

"It wasn't a dressing-down. You are not to be thinking so, indeed," Eleanor protested. "How should I be so rude and ungrateful as to . . . when Cecily has been a perfect angel to me? Cecily explained that there are people in town responsible for that sort of thing, which didn't seem to quite— But then, she hasn't minded at all that I continue to do a little plain sewing of my own when we are at home, so that's all right."

"When you are at home? But that isn't often, by all accounts," he supplied helpfully.

"Indeed no," said Eleanor, instantly diverted. "I think we must have been to every ball and soiree in London. I don't know to this day what made you persuade Mama to let me come, but I've been wanting to thank you forever! And after telling me, too, that you don't like helping people." Her eyes danced with enthusiasm.

"But has it answered?" he asked dampeningly. "Remember you came to town for a purpose, Miss Needwood. Mr. Fienne said that your mama has been called home, but won't she expect you to return with a husband?"

"I have a feeling Mama will have you up before a magistrate before too long for breach of promise!" said Eleanor, grinning. "I seem to *know* everyone, but your predictions of gentlemen—or at least of *eligible* gentlemen—lining up for me were sadly exaggerated."

He coughed. "You know, Miss Needwood, I've a dreadful feel that I know why that should be!"

She looked at him expectantly.

"Everyone thinks you are to marry me, and that is why you have received no offers!"

Eleanor did not even bother to correct his erroneous impression that she had no admirers; indeed, she was so surprised to learn that he knew about the marriage rumors, and so busy readjusting her ideas about him, that she did not immediately reply at all. Seeing her silenced for once, Lord Markham went on to say, in a gentle way, kindly meant, "I know it will be a shock to you, but you had better find out from me than someone else, to my way of thinking."

Unpredictably, Eleanor broke into a gurgle of laughter.

He raised his quizzing glass. "I really don't see what's so funny," he said, annoyed by what appeared to him to be extraordinary levity, even for *her*.

"I'm sorry, but it's *you*," she replied, still laughing. "It's your expression that's so funny. All that mystery and I know better than thouing, when actually you don't! I know all about the rumors, for your sister told me days ago, and I was just wondering how to tell you. Though I admit that it's no laughing matter."

"I should think not, indeed. It's a devil of a coil to find ourselves in."

"You mean you don't *want* to marry me?"

Startled, he looked up to find her face full of mischief.

"That tongue will get you into trouble one of these days, my girl," he predicted crossly.

Meekly she apologized and folded her hands in her lap, peeping out at him from beneath the poke of her very fetching promenade bonnet, her cheeks dimpling with the effort of maintaining a prim mouth.

"Miss Needwood, you have become a flirt!"

"I'm afraid I *have*," she agreed, which piece of honesty made them both laugh and soon had them much in charity with each other.

Spotting some beds of spring flowers just off the path, Lord Markham suggested they take a stroll, and having thrown his reins to his tiger, he helped her down.

"What *did* make you take my side against Mama that day?" asked Eleanor as they wandered among the flower beds.

"Heaven knows," he replied with a terse laugh. "Her self-satisfied expression, I think."

"Oh, yes. That is just Mama. But how disappointing. I had hoped it was because you liked, and wished, to help me. Oh, no! I forgot. You don't *like* helping people, do you?"

"Perhaps I should have taken you to Sir Maltby's castle myself! He'd have soon smoothed off that tongue of yours."

"Perhaps you should have," Eleanor agreed indulgently. "But never fear. Mama has managed, with her usual aplomb, to keep him dangling after me in case I can't catch anyone else. Really, one cannot help admiring her skill even while one is appalled by it. So if you can't bear to have me about, it isn't too late. And I can certainly see that it would make things more comfortable for you."

"Things could hardly be more uncomfortable, could they, with all these rumors flying about. And heaven knows who could have started 'em. Do *you* know?"

"I? Goodness me, no. How should I know?" Eleanor said, her voice ringing with hurt innocence.

Fortunately Lord Markham's attention had just then been claimed by a particularly fine shrub just coming into flower, and he failed to notice a slight rosiness spread out over Eleanor's cheeks. For in truth, now that she had had leisure to consider it, Eleanor had worked out for herself from whence must have originated the rumors, though Cecy would die rather than admit it.

"Well, it's deuced awkward for both of us, and there's no denying that," said Markham, unconsciously batting the head of a long clump of grass with his cane.

"You need not be depressed. Now that you are in town, I shall simply tell everyone that they have entirely mistaken the matter, which is what I wished to do from the start. Your sister was against it, and I let myself be persuaded, but I can see that you are upset about it and I'll not have you annoyed in such a way, when you've already done so much for me."

Since that had been precisely what he had been hoping she would suggest, it unnerved him to find himself so unwilling to have her rush into it. She must be made to see that the situation needed rather more sensitive handling than simply to blurt out the truth to everyone. Feeling his way, he said kindly, "You know, for once Cecy was in the right of it. She understands the seriousness of our situation, which I think *you* do not." He had expected her expression to alter into something like comprehension, but seeing her maintain a very pragmatic calm, he knew that he must have been too vague. With such a downright person as Miss Needwood, it would be necessary to be blunt. "Perhaps I should have said that Cecy understands better than you do the seriousness of *your* situation?"

She looked up at him, still uncomprehending for about ten seconds, then, with a deep blush said, "I collect that you mean that society would tend to give *you* the benefit of the doubt and *shun* me. Well, and so it would. I am not so much of a ninnyhammer as not to realize that. You are the heir to an earldom and I am a nobody. A relative nobody, at all events."

He tried to protest, but she put up her hand. "No, it is as I say. How should that prevent me from doing what is right? It would be wicked to have you inconvenienced because I lacked resolution. Of all things, *that* is what I most despise. I shall go at once to Lady Castlereagh and tell her that the betrothal never was. I shall say that I have no idea how the rumor started, and if she doesn't choose to believe it, so be it. She can tell the other patronesses at Almack's and all London will know by tomorrow."

Touched by her courage, he found himself wondering why he should not simply accept the sacrifice. Would it mean so very much to her? London wasn't her usual stamping ground as it was his: She could very easily pack her things and go home. And if it had to be with her crest lowered, it would be but a brief disgrace. It would certainly be the most convenient way of dealing with the situation. To his surprise, he heard himself saying, "I can't let you do that, Miss Needwood. Don't you realize that if we announce that we aren't to be married after all, it won't be a five-minute scandal and then everything as it was before? You'll be ruined!"

"Ruined! Oh—I did not precisely realize—" She

62

squared her shoulders. "Well, that is my problem, sir. You've done enough already."

"It is not only *your* problem, so don't be so haughty! I'm as much in this as you are. If anyone cries off, it must be thought to be you! I insist on it!"

"You insist! No, indeed, sir, I won't. Why, then *you'd* look foolish."

"Can't be helped."

"I *won't* cry off. There must be another way."

"If there is, I don't see it."

"Well, that's not very surprising: You're a man," she said sagely. "Women are far more devious. If you won't let me confess to Lady Castlereagh, it seems to me that we couldn't do better than to let things stand for the moment. Not have you telling everyone I've jilted you! Something is bound to present itself. We are not idiots. We are certain to think up some plan or other, or to find that something unexpected occurs that makes it a simple matter to explain things without either of us being blamed."

"I'd no idea you were such an optimist. What could *possibly* explain this fiasco?"

"I don't know! Anything might!"

"How long do you suggest we keep up the pretense? If we go on much longer, surely it'll only make matters worse. Whatever will people think?"

"They'll think we are going to be betrothed, just as we intend," she said with unanswerable logic, "though it will mean, of course, that we'll have to behave as if we're lovers, which will be a bore. But at least you won't have to make love to me unless someone else is around. I know how you hate exerting yourself! I should think we'll be perfectly comfortable, don't you?"

"Oh, perfectly. How could we be anything else?"

She looked at him doubtfully. "You *can* manage to play the lover for a few weeks, I suppose?"

"I'll just have to try my very hardest, won't I?" he said humbly.

"That was unhandsome of me, wasn't it? I am sure you'll do it really well."

"You are too kind."

"Not at all," she said pleasantly. "We've got to be nice to each other, haven't we? After all, people will expect to see us together every day if they are to believe we love each other. Shall you be able to bear it? You don't mind *too* much, do you?"

"Mind, Miss Needwood? How can you ask?"

"Well, I'm glad of that, at all events. I should tell you that I mean to make use of you shamefully in getting on the right side of all the best people. I know how you hate being useful, but I think it's good for you!"

CHAPTER

8

On his way next morning for a few practice rounds at Gentleman Jackson's pugilistic school, Lord Markham suddenly remembered his obligation to Miss Needwood, and turned his carriage instead up Grosvenor Street into the square.

When he entered his sister's drawing room, he found that he was by no means the first to pay a morning call, for besides Lady Sefton and Lady Castlereagh, already comfortably ensconced in Lady Cecily's peacock-covered chairs, one of Miss Needwood's most ardent admirers had dropped in to bring her a posy of fresh primroses, for he had heard her telling Lady Cecily at the opera house on the previous evening how she missed the hedgerows at home, which would now be full of them. Mr. Orlando Fairfax had first seen Miss Needwood some weeks before: seen her, and stayed to admire, having decided in a blinding moment that she must be his. He was a very romantic young gentleman, handsome in an effeminate way, with long, wispy pale hair, and a pair of pleading brown eyes that made Eleanor think of her spaniel at home. A gentleman of some means, Mr. Fairfax yet did not squander his time, for, someone having once admired one of his youthful paintings, he fancied himself an artist, and had come to affect an air and a way of dressing himself that he hoped informed the world of it. He snapped his fingers at Brummell's teachings of neatness and propriety. Not for him immaculate coats that fitted like a second skin, requiring a servant to force them on. He scorned such fripperies. His own coats were loose and flowing, with rolled collars and large buttons, and he wore them over baggy Cossack trousers, pleated at the waist, for a more sensitive appearance. At his neck hung a large floppy white silk bow above a watered-silk waistcoat, arranged with the watch chain and fobs without which he would have felt naked. He never wore boots, always light stockings and shoes with ribbon bows, even during the day, and he sat now, on a cushion at Eleanor's feet, apparently lost in rapt contemplation of them, holding one of his feet a little in the air and wiggling his toes about.

The reason for his abstraction was clear: Lady Castlereagh was holding forth to the assembled company upon some matter of policy, and Mr. Fairfax felt neglected.

"I am beginning to be seriously displeased," pontificated this most starchy of Almack's patronesses, "by the unfortunate tendency for our young men to appear in trousers at our Wednesday assemblies!" As she spoke, she raised her quizzing glass and stared pointedly at the splendid pair that adorned Orlando's shapely legs. "They are unhappy garments at best, and quite unsuited to people of fashion."

In her gentle voice Lady Sefton said quietly, "You know, my dear, one cannot help but sympathize. Only think how much easier to wear they are. Nobody denies the elegance of knee breeches, but I have often thought how trying they must be for those with less than perfect calves."

"There is always wadding! My father never went out without wadding in his life, and I never heard *him* complain. And why should not men, too, put themselves out for fashion? I suppose today's low necklines are easy to wear? A person with style overcomes such minor irritations. I've found that one may always manage to achieve a creditable appearance without going beyond the pale."

Mr. Fairfax, who had been sadly put out by her attack on his beloved Cossacks, muttered audibly under his breath, "From what I've seen, I'd say that quite a few don't manage it at all!"

Lady Castlereagh, already irritated by his unaccountable behavior in lounging all over her hostess's floor, turned to him coldly. "I beg your pardon, Mr. Fairfax. I did not quite hear—"

Mr. Fairfax raised seraphic eyes. "I was only thinking, ma'am, that if Almack's obliged us in the matter of trousers, several of us would be more than happy to encourage *some* ladies, at least, to cover up, if they are more comfortable to do so. One or two I can think of give us all a devilish turn."

Lady Castlereagh ignored such a pointed attack on her sex and turned back to Lady Sefton. "As I was saying, my dear, I do think we should add a rule as to trousers, and the doorman shall enforce it. There is nobody more firm than Mr. Willis in keeping out undesirables."

"I'm sure I would not like . . ." Lady Sefton began to say uncomfortably.

"What about those poor unfortunates with knock knees?" pursued the unrepentant Mr. Fairfax. "Wad-

67

ding's no help there. Rather mean if you ask me. Must quite ruin a fellow's evening to show 'em off!" He glanced up at Eleanor for approval, but seeing her looking determinedly elsewhere, only the tiniest quiver of her lip showing that his remarks had found their mark, he turned back to his adversary at once, an eyebrow cocked to suggest that he for one was perfectly prepared to pursue further such an interesting line of discussion.

It was at that moment that Lady Cecily's footman announced Lord Markham, and his sister was not alone in greeting his arrival with relief.

Only one visitor was uninterested in seeing him turn up in Grosvenor Square, for Mr. Fairfax never listened to gossip and was quite unaware that Markham was being hotly tipped to carry off his love from under his nose. As for the others, they were most unaffectedly interested in seeing how Lord Markham greeted Miss Needwood. Nor did he disappoint them, for with a friendly nod to the others he crossed the room, and bowing low over Eleanor's hand, kissed it with the ardency of a man deprived of manna, first stepping carefully round Mr. Fairfax, at whom he threw a hard stare. Eleanor twinkled up at him, and Lady Sefton, mistaking her expression for something warmer, caught Lady Castlereagh's eye conspiratorially.

It was obvious from Lord Markham's appearance that he did not intend to stay, for he carried with him his high-crowned beaver, and his many-caped drabcoat still hung from his shoulders. Leaving Eleanor for a moment, he went to join his sister, perching himself on the arm of her chair. Planting a brotherly tribute on her cheek, he said in a voice meant for everyone, "You know who I'm after, Cecy, so I won't attempt to cozen you. Will it sink me if I beg to be allowed to take Miss Needwood for a drive in my curricle? She promised me yesterday that I might do so."

Eleanor blushed becomingly; Lady Castlereagh spoke for the whole company in encouraging him not to stand on ceremony, and in only a few minutes Eleanor found herself driving away with him along Upper Brook Street toward Hyde Park, with Mr. Fairfax's protests still ringing in her ears.

"That was prettily done, sir," said Eleanor once he had steadied his horses.

"Thank you, Miss Needwood. I'm glad you are pleased with me," he said docilely.

"Who said I'm pleased with you? I'm not at all. Where were you last night? I did *tell* you we were going to the opera, didn't I?"

"You didn't tell me you expected to see *me* there!" he said in horror. "I *never* go to the opera. Can't abide all that caterwauling."

"I don't like it, either, but your sister arranged it, and on your first full day back in town everyone will have expected you to spend the evening with me! It was not at all well done of you, sir, though you've probably re-established our credibility this morning. I must say your timing was immaculate! Lady Castlereagh *and* Lady Sefton. It could not be better!"

"Haven't you forgotten the young man who was tying your shoe riband?"

"Mr. Fairfax! Isn't he diverting? You just missed hearing him come to cuffs with Lady Castlereagh about his unmentionables. I promise you would have enjoyed it."

"Affected young puppy! What were you doing, encouraging him to languish at your feet like that?"

"Oh, it's perfectly proper. Apparently in artistic circles it's all the crack to seat oneself on cushions."

"Is that where he fancies himself? Artistic circles? Then that explains the floppy bow. Still, I'm not sure you should encourage him to sit at your feet. I wonder why he does it."

"Because he thinks he's in love with me, of course. He wants to paint me."

"Au naturel, I shouldn't wonder, with someone like him."

"I say, do you think so? What a lark."

She seemed so much taken by the idea that the viscount, who had begun to have serious misgivings about leaving his future in Eleanor's hands, made a mental note to keep a better guard on his tongue. He contented himself with saying merely, "Well, I hardly think it would answer if you *did* let him paint you, since you want people to believe that *we* are betrothed. They'd know that I should not allow a rival that privilege."

"Where are you taking me, sir?" Eleanor asked, pulling the rug more closely around her knees. "Is it Hyde Park, because if it is, I'd rather not. I need to have a serious talk with you. I've a splendid idea how to rid ourselves of our problem, but if we go into the park we will see everyone we know and then we won't get a chance to talk."

"Where then, Miss Needwood?"

"If you please, I'd like to go to Mr. Bullock's Museum."

He turned to her with a glazed expression.

"It's in Piccadilly," she told him helpfully.

"I know *where* it is. I just didn't realize that people actually *went* there."

"Haven't you been there, either? Oh, lovely, then it'll be quite a treat. My sister Lizzie has read all about it—she's the clever one of Stepmama's girls—and in her last letter she said I was on no account to miss it!"

"Oh, no, you mustn't do that," he agreed weakly.

"I must admit that I was a little embarrassed about asking you to take me," confided Eleanor. "For there is nothing worse than being obliged to go over places one has already visited. But now that I know that you haven't been there, either, I can be perfectly easy, for only show me the gentleman who is not interested in weapons and armor and stuffed elephants and things!"

Lord Markham thought he could show her several, but patiently turned his vehicle back the way they had come while Eleanor informed him with every sign that she considered it to be chiefly to his benefit, that in Bullock's they would be able to have a really comfortable coze, as she was sure they wouldn't see anyone they knew. It was an assurance Lord Markham could only share, since he could not conceive of any circumstance that might lure any of his friends to such a place, and he entered the columned entrance without any other misgiving than the threat of boredom.

"It says here that this is *one of the most refined, rational, and interesting exhibitions the metropolis has ever witnessed*," said Eleanor, referring to a small guidebook produced from her reticule.

"I say, do put that thing away," said the viscount hurriedly. "Do you want the world to think we are provincials?"

"But I *am* a provincial, sir," she giggled.

71

"Not when you're with me," he said firmly, slipping the little volume into his pocket and tucking Miss Needwood's arm in his.

Impatient as was the viscount to hear Eleanor's idea, she would not even think of sitting down with him until she had seen all the exhibits, and he was obliged to endure quite an hour and a half in which she minutely studied everything she saw, for, as she told him confidentially, Lizzie would expect from her a full and detailed description on her return home. While the viscount could find little to interest him in the multitude of glass cases of stuffed birds and mammals lining the walls under the glass cupola, he was mildly interested in two suits of armor, and became quite enthusiastic at seeing the military carriage of the late emperor Napoleon Bonaparte. He was even willing to be impressed by the basaltic cavern and the Indian hut, but finally put his foot down when they came upon a set piece in which, wrapped around the trunks of some palm trees that shaded some dozen or so stuffed wild animals, several large pythons had been made to writhe artfully amid the foliage in a way that quite made his flesh creep!

Persuading Eleanor that she had seen enough to write home about, he led her to a rectangular stone slab that served instead of a bench, and she sat down cautiously, uneasily aware that over her shoulder a fierce-looking zebra appeared to be ready to charge.

Flicking out his coattails, Markham sat beside her and begged her to outline her scheme. Her answer unnerved him somewhat.

"How good are you at acting, Lord Markham?"

He groaned, but preferring not to hear him, she went

72

on cheerfully. "I have a simply marvelous plan. It came to me last night when I was reading one of Mrs. Radcliffe's stories, and I knew at once that it would be just the thing."

"Do go on. I cannot wait to hear what you have thought up for me."

"I knew you were a right one," approved Eleanor, "which is just as well, for you will know just how to get hold of the footpads we shall need."

"Which footpads would those be?" he asked in hollow tones.

"The ones who are going to attack you, of course. Though they won't be real footpads, naturally."

"You relieve my mind, ma'am. I can't tell you how much."

"Relieve your— Oh! You are joking me!"

"Not, I assure you! Naturally, I pass over any slur on my character that suggests that I am so steeped in infamy that I should know exactly how to get hold of a gang of footpads. Tell me, what is this plan?"

"I can tell by your voice that you think it will be foolish, but it is actually perfectly straightforward. All you have to do is pretend to be attacked by footpads, who will rob and then hit you on the head, leaving you unconscious."

"Oh, is *that* all! Good heavens, and I thought you were going to ask me to do something unpleasant!"

"Don't be silly. They won't *really* hit you. And when you wake up—well, you won't have been unconscious, will you, so you can't really wake up, but you know what I mean—when you *pretend* to wake up, you will say that you have lost your memory."

"And I am sure that will be entirely delightful, but how does it help?"

"I'm coming to that, naturally. When I come to visit you on your sickbed, you must look at me with a dreamy expression, and then astound everyone by saying that you don't know who I am. *Now* do you understand? Naturally, I shall be hurt. Mortified! And then I shall say in a heartrending little voice that if you cannot remember me, I see I have no option but to give you your freedom. And I shall be so tender, so affecting, that nobody will dream that it is a take-in."

"But that means I'll have to pretend to lose my memory forever!"

"Why does it?"

"Well, if I got it back again, everyone would expect me to come after you, wouldn't they?"

"Oh! I didn't think of that." She hesitated. "You don't think you could keep up the pretense—"

"No!" he said firmly, his lips twitching. "I do not!"

"And it was such a good idea. Are you absolutely sure you could not—"

"Miss Needwood, I said no!"

"Well, all right, sir. Don't be so uppity. It was only my first idea, after all. I am sure I shall soon think of something else."

"Such promises have flattened lesser men."

She laughed without umbrage, and sat wrapped in contemplation as scheme after improbable scheme chased across her imagination.

The viscount sat watching her, and after a few minutes said reflectively, "How is it that each time I see you, you appear more beautiful than when I saw you last?"

She reddened. "You don't have to say pretty things to me when we are on our own, you know. Only in front of others."

"Oh, but I have to practice," he said lightly. "You may think me a silver-tongued Lothario, but even a man of my address must keep his hand in."

She giggled, glad that he had been joking. "Then I promise faithfully to take none of your extravagant compliments seriously, how is that, sir?"

"Come, Miss Needwood," he said, feeling oddly resentful. "I think it's time I returned you to my sister before you destroy my confidence altogether. But I shall do my duty and see you tonight at Lady Castlereagh's ball. It'll be a devilish squeeze. Will you save me a dance?"

"I shall save you *two*, sir," she said severely. "Do you want people to say you are going off me?"

"Who would believe that anyone could fall out of love with the beautiful Miss Needwood?"

"I know you said you need to practice, sir, but don't lay it on so thick, sir, I pray."

"What an ingrate you are, child!"

Feeling strangely unsettled, having dropped Eleanor at his sister's house, Lord Markham drove himself back to St. James's Square. Entering his house, he noticed a familiar stick lying on the hall table next to a hat and some leather gloves. Before Fulmer, his butler, could say so much as a word, he had pushed past him into the library.

"Good Lord, Fulmer, it's just as I thought!" he cried, pausing on the threshold. "Haven't I told you not to open up my rooms to all the riffraff in town?"

Neither Fulmer, who knew the visitor very well, nor the object of this pleasantry, were in the least offended and, with a smile that made his eyes sparkle, the intruder had covered the distance between them and was shaking Markham by the hand and pumping his shoulder so heartily that the viscount was moved to protest with a broad grin, "I say, old fellow, the coat! It's the first time I've had it on!"

His friend ceased his ministrations to Markham's shoulder and eyed the coat doubtfully. "Well, that's something, at all events. But if you've really been going about this morning in that thing, I've arrived not a moment too soon!"

"Damn you, Francis, but it's good to see you," replied the viscount without rancor, "even if you don't know what you're talking about when it comes to coats."

"Don't know what I'm talking about? Me? Even Brummell's coats never fitted like mine!"

"And he took good care not to let 'em." Markham laughed. "And look at this thing!" he went on, flicking at the spotted Belcher handkerchief his guest wore instead of a cravat. "You look like a coachman."

"Corinthian, if you don't mind, my friend! I'll have you know it takes ages to achieve just the right blend of smart and casual."

"Take my word for it, you haven't!" said Markham, touching the side of his nose.

Fulmer, who had been looking on indulgently, ventured to ask his master if Mr. Francis would be staying to luncheon.

"Staying to luncheon? Of course he is, man. And dinner, too, if we can persuade him!"

The Honorable Mr. Francis Hervey was perhaps Lord Markham's oldest friend. Indeed, their fathers had been great friends before them, and they had known each other as boys, cementing their affection first at Eton and then at Oxford, where it had been said of them that never before had a duo brought idleness to such a pitch of perfection. Mr. Hervey, an engaging rascal, had the dark, well-defined good looks much loved of the ladies. He flirted with every one of them he met, and he went through life causing so much havoc within maidenly bosoms that some parents had gone so far as to warn off their daughters despite his handsome fortune. Not a man of intellect, he was, like Lord Markham, a keen sportsman. A bruising rider to hounds, a member of both the Four-in-Hand and the Pugilist Club, he entered vigorously into the proceedings at any convivial gathering of like-minded men. He had a boyish sense of humor that made him the prime mover in practical jokes, and though of late Markham had once or twice thought some of his schemes a trifle adolescent (as on the memorable occasion when he had released a monkey at one of Mrs. Drummond-Burrell's select soirees), he couldn't help but be amused by the enthusiasm with which he pursued them. Nor was he sorry to see him in town, for there were few people he thought better company.

"Where are you staying, old fellow?" Markham asked once they were snugly ensconced around a decanter. "It goes without saying that you are welcome here."

"Can't be done, much as I'd like to. Staying in Cavendish Square with Mama. M'sister's come-out, don't you know. Mama has dragged us all to town for it, just as I'd caught a whiff of a fight being staged up near

Harrogate. But Ma says it's m'duty, as the heir, at least to see her safely through the early part of the season, so I can't let her down, though what she supposes I shall do that m'father can't, I've no idea. Not that I'd let my little Letty down, as you can imagine."

"What? Is it *Letty's* come-out? What, *little Letty*? Good Lord! Seems only yesterday she was in short skirts. Mind you, she's a sweet little thing. Thought so last time I saw her. I should think she'd take. Especially with *her* dowry."

"With her dowry, a one-eyed donkey would take! Only hope she finds someone she can like into the bargain."

Pouring himself a generous glass of port, he suddenly remembered he had a grievance. "And talking about dowries, I've a bone to pick with you. A fine state of affairs when my best friend gets betrothed and I'm the last to hear of it."

"If you're talking about me, you're miles out!"

"Don't give me that. The whole town is buzzing with it."

"Then they shouldn't be."

"You mean you're not engaged to this Miss Needwood I've heard so much about?"

"No, I'm not," said Markham, rather puzzled as to what Miss Needwood would wish him to say but not willing for his friend to get the wrong end of the stick. He briefly debated with himself whether he should tell Francis the whole story, but decided that Francis was rather too free with his tongue to be trusted and left it at that.

"You mean you haven't come to the point?" said Francis gleefully. "Even you are not so idle."

Again Markham was tempted to tell him the truth, but recollected that the secret was not only his. "Idle or not, I assure you I haven't," he said calmly, "though Miss Needwood is a charming girl."

"She's leaving you dangling! By all that's rich! I never thought to hear of a woman with sense. I've half a mind to take her from under your nose for being so hamfisted. From what I've heard, she's a rare beauty."

"Feel free, old man," said Markham, half exasperated by the coil he was getting into. "I've no claim on her."

CHAPTER

9

Lady Castlereagh could not have been happier about the timing of her first ball of the season, and was entertained with beautiful visions of Lady Jersey having to watch Markham and Miss Needwood meet in society for the first time under a rival's roof.

If the elite company assembled expected them to arrive together, it was disappointed: Miss Needwood came with the Fiennes, and by the time Markham entered the ballroom, she was already dancing with Mr. Fairfax.

Yet to be presented, Eleanor was simply dressed in a white figured-silk gown ornamented with a falling lace tucker, and pearls. When Lady Cecily saw her, she hugged her to her impulsively, only to think how beautiful Markham must think her.

Cecily had watched very carefully their meeting in the park and was beginning to feel quite hopeful. If he didn't like her, why would he take her off in such a conspicuous manner? And she knew that Eleanor had saved him two dances.

Had Eleanor noticed Markham's entry to the ball, she would certainly have been gratified at the way *he* stared when he saw her. But others *had* noticed, and drew their own conclusions.

Smiling to himself, Markham watched her progress down the set, reflecting on how right he had been to persuade Mrs. Needwood to give Eleanor her season in town. She danced well, he noted with approval, and had a stately air in the ballroom quite at variance with her usual scampish behavior. *Let us hope she manages to keep that tongue clamped between those pretty white teeth,* he thought, laughing quietly to himself, quite unaware of the impression he was creating.

His eyes ranged over the dancers to find out who else was there. His sister was dancing with De Lieven, the Russian ambassador, and knowing that Hartley danced only with his wife, he peered across heads to find him. He was on the other side of the room among a group being served champagne by a footman, and reminded of his own thirst, Markham went to move their way, when a voice at his side delayed him.

"So, you *are* in town, Markham. I'd heard you were. How exquisite of you to come and see me!"

"Violet!" He managed to inject into his voice a modicum of enthusiasm. "What a pleasant surprise."

"How much of a surprise can it be, Markham?" drawled the lady. "You had my note."

"Did you leave a note? I didn't know. Fulmer must have forgotten to give it to me."

"Oh, no, Markham. How unhandsome of you, blaming the excellent Fulmer."

Reflecting briefly on the unwisdom of allowing her to become so conversant with his butler's virtues, he admitted reluctantly that the fault was entirely his own and delivered a handsome apology and a smile that he

81

intended to be conciliatory. It seemed instead to inflame her.

"I suppose you have been too busy, since you came up to town?"

Too indolent to enjoy dealing with an angry woman, he would have liked to have moved away, only he could not find a way of taking his leave of her without being rude, he stood with her for several minutes, making desultory conversation, though he could not prevent his attention from wandering. While Lady Violet tried to attract him back to her, he unconsciously fixed his eyes upon Eleanor, still dancing with Mr. Fairfax. His interest in the girl infuriated the woman at his side.

"I see you watch Miss Needwood. What a pity that she does not realize how pert people think her," she drawled, too angry to be wise. "There is something quite audacious in her speech, which it is impossible to like. So *coming* for a young girl: her opinions so fixed and not at all what one finds pleasing. Really, it is quite a puzzle to see what there is to admire."

"Not to me, it isn't," said Markham tactlessly. "I think her handsome."

"Handsome? Miss Needwood? Oh, forgive me, my dear. I'd no idea she was such a favorite. Your tastes must certainly have altered this past year."

He considered for a moment. "Do you know, I really think they *have*," he said cheerfully, and pausing only to give her arm a consoling little pat, he passed into the body of the ballroom, leaving the lady to fume at his back as he made his way over to Hartley.

Lady Violet Pelham was not used to such cavalier treatment, especially from men, by whom she was used, invariably, to hearing herself described as a fine figure of a woman. It was not difficult to understand why, for she was possessed of the luxuriant figure and seductive features many men mistake for beauty. Built on majestic lines, she was careful never to offend the decencies by overexposing them, having no disposition to forfeit her place among the ton. She wore her gowns décolleté, as fashion decreed; but she was not among those who damped down their skirts to make them cling to thighs and legs and show off handsome figures. She followed none of the excesses practiced by more sensational society ladies, but she looked the sort who might, and while men had imaginations, it was enough.

Among the ton her history was thought unusual enough to be interesting, for she had lived most of her life in India, her father and her husband having been leading lights in the East India Company, an orbit she had loathed, albeit luxuriously, with a supreme resentment. During her husband's lifetime she had desired with the fiercest of passions to free herself from the Indian subcontinent, and far from being the end of her hopes, her husband's premature death, from a common Indian fever, had been the beginning. She had determined at once on coming home and taking her place among the beau monde, assisted by her husband's clever investments in the despised country, which had yielded a lavish fortune.

Her initial period of mourning was spent in selling up to her best advantage, and it was some eighteen months later in London, when she was being fitted for her first dress of half-mourning, that she first had a glimmer of an idea as to how to make society notice her. The dress was of deep mauve silk, a color she naturally associated with death and had never worn. As she saw herself in it for the first time, she was surprised at how well she looked and was struck by a strange fancy. She determined at once that her name would project her image. Taking care to find the precise shade of violet to best suit her, she had had an exquisite wardrobe in that single shade made up for her at Stagg and Mantle's in Leicester Square. As an adjunct, she decided, too, that she would always wear about her person the perfume of the flower whose name she bore. The ton loved idiosyncrasy and took her up: Men called her the Violet Lady; ladies followed her strange fashion for a sufficient period to launch her triumphantly. It had delighted her vanity to drive women into half-mourning in emulation, and by the time that satisfaction had worn thin and she had all but abandoned it, she was too much known to be ignored, especially where the gentlemen were concerned. Quickly at home in London society, she soon decided that she was not interested in another marriage: Once had been enough for that. Now she was free to enjoy the excitement of the chase and a wild brief moment instead of the humdrum of the marriage bed. She had had no lack of takers for what she had to offer in such abundance, but recently Markham had driven off all opposition for an ecstatic month: All the more strange that he should now neglect her. She really had no desire to take up with him again on the old terms, but it was not her way to lose her men ungrudgingly, and as she watched him walk away from her, a calculating look marred her beauty just for a moment.

Hartley viewed Markham's coming with misgiving, having been earlier charged by his wife to ascertain how matters stood between her brother and Eleanor. Hartley had much rather stay out of it, but when he said as much to Cecily, she accused him of heartlessness, professed that if he could be so indifferent to the fate of her dearest Markham, then he could not really love *her*, and had finally succumbed, when she had not seemed to be getting her way, to a bout of tears. Even less devoted men might not have been proof against such powerful persuasion. He had reluctantly promised to do his utmost to elicit the true state of affairs from Markham, his wife having earlier failed miserably in her own attempts at interrogating Eleanor.

Markham was always popular, and for a few moments was swallowed up by the men who stood around Hartley, but he reached him at last, and they were soon exchanging views on the miseries of such a squeeze. Hartley could not help noticing, while they were talking, how preoccupied in watching Eleanor he was, and took his opportunity while it offered.

"Fine girl, that," he said with a casual air that would not have deceived Markham for a moment if he'd been paying attention.

As it was, his mind continued fixed on Eleanor, and he answered only, "Mmm. Charming," a dearth of words highly unsatisfactory to Mr. Fienne at such a moment.

"You took Miss Needwood off for a drive this morning," he persevered. "Where'd you go? Hyde Park?"

Markham's attention was at once removed from Eleanor to Hartley, at whom he glared. "Why? What's she been saying?"

"Good heavens, what on earth *should* she have been saying? I'm only asking a civil question."

Seeing Hartley's usual bovine expression, Markham knew that he had jumped to wrong conclusions: But, anyway, with Eleanor in Hartley's house, he could not expect to hide from him his visit to Bullock's. Changing color rather, he said casually, "We were both weary of the park, matter of fact. Fancied a bit of a change, so we went to Bullock's. The museum in Piccadilly, you know."

Hartley stared at him in fascinated horror and then, a half minute later, said faintly, "Sorry! Thought you said Bullock's Museum just for a moment there."

Markham's color deepened. "That's it! Devil of a fine museum. Don't know when I've been more pleased with a place."

As far as Hartley was concerned, there was really nothing more to be said. He'd never really trusted Cecily's intuition, but if Miss Needwood had enough about her to lure Markham to Bullock's, it must be only a hop and a jump to church, and he tactfully dropped a subject that he, at least, found acutely embarrassing, fully confident that he could report favorably to his wife on progress.

He picked up another thread of conversation, remarking, "Francis is in town, don't you know, Markham. Saw him this morning."

"I saw him myself, matter of fact," said Markham cheerfully. "Poor old fellow says he's going to be tied up the whole season with Letty's come-out. Devil of a business. Mother depending on him to do the pretty."

"No! Poor old soul. These women! It'll mean the opera, I daresay. Balls, soirees. Ttt!" He shook his head. "A bad business."

"We'll have to see if we can cheer him up a bit. Get him across the heavy ground as light as possible."

"Good thinking."

"Mind you, he's got his own plans. Thinking of getting up a flirtation with Miss Needwood to while away the time."

Hartley stared rather bleakly for a moment. "Won't that queer your pitch a bit?" he said, puzzled.

"No. Why should it?" Markham replied, equally puzzled.

"Thought you and she were, well, you know . . ."

"Oh, don't you start, Hart. You of all people know there's nothing between us."

"Well, so I should have *thought*, old man. But Cecy seems very convinced there *is*. And then, you did take her to Bullock's."

"I didn't *want* to go to Bullock's, you idiot! Couldn't get out of it once she was in my curricle."

"But Cecy said when you collected her you were all over the girl!"

Markham went to try to explain, looked at Hartley's rather vacuous expression, and gave up. "Take my word for it, there's *nothing* between us! And if Francis wants to get up a flirtation with the girl, he's more than welcome!"

For Hartley it was a revelation, and as the Russian ambassador returned Cecily to his side, he looked for an opportunity to tell his wife that plans were not quite going as she hoped. To his dismay, Markham lingered by them, and he racked his brain to think of a way to speak to his wife without him overhearing.

Eleanor, too, was being led back by her partner, Mr. Fairfax, but seeing her detained by another admirer, obviously seeking the favor of a dance, and seeing how beautiful she looked between the two men, Lady Cecily could not miss an opportunity to draw her to Markham's attention.

"Only look, brother, at how cross Mr. Fairfax is with Veren for trying to cut him out! How fond of Miss Needwood he seems, to be sure. And what a handsome pair they'd make."

Now, Hartley, big with new information, saw at once what she was at and, pretending to scratch his nose, shook his head frantically from side to side, hoping to catch his wife's attention. In this he was successful since both Cecy and Markham stared at him for a moment before continuing their conversation.

"That fop!" sneered her brother in disgust. "Just look at him! Wearing those Cossack bags in a ballroom!"

"Oh, but anything passes these days, Markham."

"Bad tailoring never passes in any day. I'd be surprised to hear that Miss Needwood admires him so much as he admires himself. Look at that way he has of flicking back his pretty curls. Affected puppy."

"Oh, no, Markham, you're too harsh! He's artistic, merely. All his set have long hair. And I refuse to call into doubt his admiration of Miss Needwood. Why, he wants to paint her portrait."

"She isn't really going to sit for *him*, surely?"

"Why not? I'm told he paints quite well. Madame de Lieven sat for him last year, and she says that the portrait is very like."

"Who could not achieve a creditable likeness of Dorothea? Even I could take a respectable stab at that sharp nose and long neck. It would take something more to catch Miss Needwood. Laurence, perhaps, might do it, but not that ninny."

"I suppose you will say that the Marquess of Veren is

a ninny, too, brother," she said archly, nodding over to where Eleanor's other admirer was still trying to cut him out.

But Markham could say no such thing, for it was a plain fact that everyone liked the marquess, a lively but sweet-natured young man in his late twenties who had somehow managed to remain self-effacing despite having the heavy guns of society's matrons trained on him since his come-out in their attempts to secure him, his title, and his generous fortune for one of their daughters.

"So Veren's interested now, is he?" said Markham, stroking his chin. "How long has *that* been going on?"

"Oh, she has only just met him, dearest. A week or two ago. But he certainly seems to like her."

"Strange she didn't mention him, wasn't it?"

"As if dear Nell would boast of one admirer to another," tutted his sister. "It isn't at all the thing."

"Are *you* busy with that tittle-tattle as well, Cec? For once and for all, I am *not* an admirer of Miss Needwood's. I hardly know the girl."

Such a downright statement was hardly designed to please Cecily, and she hissed peevishly, having first taken the precaution of moving away from others so that they might not be overheard, "Then why did you ask me to get the introductions? That hardly sounds like not knowing the girl."

"Cecily! Have *you* spread this dashed rumor? On the strength of my letter?"

"I? Of course not, Markham. What do you take me for? I merely obeyed your wishes."

"I didn't ask you to have her *stay* with you."

"What was I to do when her mama was sent for? You asked me to look after her."

"To get her *introductions*! That was to be the whole of your ministry on her behalf."

"Well, you never asked me to do so before, so what was I to think? It's no wonder everyone expects you to marry her."

"Everyone! For heaven's sake, girl! Who's everyone? You know, Cecy, if it *was* you who spread those rumors," he spat out furiously. "I could wring your neck!"

"I didn't!" she cried, perjuring herself indignantly. "I daresay, it was because she was such a favorite with Mama and Papa."

"Yes, and that's another thing!" said Markham, reminded of a further grievance. "Why did you introduce her to them? You might have known the old tabbies would put their heads together over that one."

"It wasn't *my* fault that Mama and Papa chose to visit me," Cecily said, pouting indignantly. "I didn't invite them."

Markham was forced to admit that he might be unfair, and added, rather more mildly, "What on earth did *they* say?"

"Oh, they *liked* Nell," said Cecily airily. "Indeed, Mama went so far as to say that she would even be pleased if you married her. And she was quite a favorite with Papa. He danced with her at Almack's."

"I don't believe you!"

"It's true! And Mama said that she would be glad to hear that you were marrying before you missed the boat—for you *are* nearly thirty! And that she could not imagine anyone more suitable than Nell."

"Good God! I'm beginning to feel hunted!"

"You should be pleased, then, if Mr. Fairfax chases after her. And as for Veren, surely he'd be quite unexceptionable."

"Oh, Veren's better than Fairfax," Markham conceded rather ungraciously, "but can you see her married into such a starchy family! His mother's a dragon!"

"La, brother! Most girls can't afford to be so choosy!"

"Most girls don't have her looks, sister!"

Even Cecily could not be displeased with such a statement after the rather unpromising conversation that went before, and she threw her husband a meaning glance just as Eleanor and her followers reached them. Eleanor, meanwhile, was still playfully depressing Lord Veren's hopes.

"No, indeed, my lord," she said, shaking her head prettily, "I cannot find you a dance. Only look at my card, if you don't believe me."

"It can't be true," cried Lord Veren equally playfully. "I won't have it. Just let me look at that card for a moment." And he snatched it from her hand before she could protest and held it out of her reach. He was a little shortsighted. "Ah, yes! Just as I suspected! Two spaces unfilled. I shall have them both, even should they turn out to be country dances."

She dimpled up at him. "But they are waltzes, sir. You wouldn't ask me to *waltz* before I've been presented? Mama won't allow me to be presented until she comes back to town. Do you want to sink me forever?"

He tapped his forehead with the heel of his hand. "Well, let me look at that card again!" His eyes darted through it. "Here! You've given Markham two dances. That's not fair! Serve him right if I took them both. Yet

91

stay. I'll be generous. I'll leave him *one*." And he crossed Markham's name through for the second of the dances Eleanor had written in for him and replaced it with his own. Lord Markham heard it all good-humoredly, for it was difficult to dislike Veren when he was being charming. Picking up from his tone, he said severely, "What's this? Taking my name in vain? Miss Needwood, I appeal to you! Is it right?"

Aware that the eyes of the entire ballroom were upon them, Eleanor, who knew that *something* would be expected of her, lowered her own eyes and blushed, as if his presence disturbed her. "Do you indeed mind so much, my lord?" she asked shyly, opening her ivory fan modestly across her bosom.

"Can you ask?" he replied with what he hoped was appropriate ardor, not taking his eyes from her face and being quite as willing as she to provide sport for their neighbors. "To be robbed of a moment must be a source of exquisite displeasure."

He saw the familiar twitch of her lips, and felt his spirits lift as he heard her murmur appreciatively, for his ears only, "Very prettily done, sir. How clever you are at all this."

He choked, fighting an overwhelming desire to laugh, but disguised it by asking thoughtlessly, and quite ruining his impression of the doting lover, "And when is our first dance, Miss Needwood? I've forgotten."

Mr. Fairfax, who continued to hover about Miss Needwood adoringly, was disgusted. "You mean you don't remember which dance Miss Needwood has kept for you? I call that a shabby thing, now. Shabby! Don't you, Veren?"

"Yes. I do."

Miss Needwood looked at Lord Markham expectantly, much as a robin might watch a person who fed him unfailingly.

He did not disappoint her. "I asked Miss Needwood for *every* dance, of course," he said gently. "I only await her pleasure in learning my reward for my perseverance. She knows that I shall dance with no other here tonight."

As Fairfax, continuing to look disappointed, followed them with his eyes, Eleanor allowed Lord Markham to lead her into the set now forming. Fully making up for his unfortunate lapse, he cleared a way through the crowd for her as if she had been a princess, and set his face in such an expression of adoration as to almost overset Eleanor's gravity.

Lord Veren's eyes narrowed meanwhile as he, too, reluctantly watched them walk away. Quite aware of the rumors circulating about Markham and Miss Needwood, it was the first time he had seen them together, and he searched their faces for signs of warmth in the hope that the rumors were without foundation.

He had returned to town rather late himself this year, and quite reluctantly. A leading light among the ton for ten years now, and as disillusioned as was Lord Markham, he scarcely expected to meet with anybody who would set wedding bells ringing in *his* ears. He had first met Miss Needwood nearly a fortnight before, and found her pretty and pleasant. He had danced with her and found her amusing. Then he had waited for the usual machinations to make him come to the point that every girl and her friends he had ever known had initiated, and for the inevitable ennui to follow. They didn't come: neither the machinations, nor the ennui. Eleanor met him two days later, perfectly cheerful, and friendly. He was pleased. She met him again, still cheerful, and he was puzzled, though he laughed at himself and called himself a coxcomb for being so.

Every time they had since met he had searched for signs that she considered him more than an acquaintance, but there were none of the distinguishing little gestures and looks he expected and now desired. Indeed, had Eleanor wished to trap him for her own, he ruefully admitted to himself, she had hit on the very scheme for bringing him to heel! But it was no scheme, of that he had reluctantly become certain. She was quite indifferent to him, his compliments, his fortune, and even his title. It was a salutary lesson and, he told himself, served him well for thinking himself such a fine fellow! It did not in any way lessen his ardor.

As for Eleanor, not only was she *not* scheming to catch the marquess himself, but it was a plain fact that she wasn't scheming, as her mama would have wished, to catch *any* of her followers. In the weeks she had been in London she had met a number of eligible suitors: There was Mr. Fairfax, of course; there had been Mr. Holbrook, whom Mama would have thought perfectly suitable since he had a house both in town and in Brighton; and then there was an Admiral Mortimer, perfectly presentable, though rather older than the others, who had made a fortune in the late wars.

And when she had told Lord Markham that none had proposed to her, she had been less than candid, for each of these gentlemen had shown unmistakable signs of being about to put the question of marriage to the test and she had been severely exercised to turn them from their purpose. Mr. Fairfax had tried to get her alone among the greenery in Lady Cecily's conservatory on more than one occasion; Mr. Holbrook had actually dropped onto one knee before, with great presence of mind, Eleanor had dashed off to help Cecily bring in refreshments; and the admiral had bent toward her so closely that his corset had creaked, with such unmistakable signs of ardor, while they were out driving in his carriage, that she had been hard put to parry his advances. And then, too, she was almost sure, there was the Marquess of Veren.

With such a choice it was surprising that Eleanor was still not betrothed. Other, less popular girls had settled their future satisfactorily during the first weeks of the season as their mamas desired. It was Eleanor's duty to do as much. She had come to town to do so, and she was as much puzzled as Lord Markham would undoubtedly have been, had he known, to understand why she did not encourage any of these gentlemen, any one of whom was a mile better than Sir Maltby, to come up to scratch. Always at the back of her mind lingered her father's words that she should choose a man harmonious to her spirit. Whoever that might be, she was fairly certain that description did not fit any of the gentlemen so far interested.

As he continued to eye her from his corner of the room, one of those interested, my lord marquess, saw with displeasure how she laughed with Lord Markham and saw on what pleasant terms they appeared to be. He ground his back teeth together miserably, but made up his mind that he would not give up so tamely.

CHAPTER

10

As soon as they were out of earshot of the others, Lord Markham asked, "Well, now, Miss Needwood, how did I do?" clearly expecting accolades.

"Not too badly, once you'd managed to overcome that disastrous slip of yours about the dancing," she conceded. "But indeed, sir, you must be sure and concentrate in the future! Fancy admitting to not knowing which dance we were to share. For shame. What kind of lover are you?"

"How *could* I be expected to know about the dances?" he asked, piqued by her criticism. "You told me only that you would save me two: You didn't say *which* two. I am not that learned pig at Bartholomew Fair that reads minds, you know."

"No, indeed," said Eleanor, biting on her lip. "I am sure you are not. Lizzie said that I must expect *him* to be like all the other little pigs, pink and with a curly tail. And clever, you know, quite clever! *He* counts, and everything!"

"Thank you, Miss Needwood! I knew I might rely on you to knock me down. To be found wanting when my direct rival is a pig must rank as the most chastening experience of my life. I wonder how many more delightful comparisons I may expect to endure before we extract ourselves from this muddle."

"None, if you like my new plan, sir," she promised, leaning confidingly toward him.

"Oh? *Another* plan? Don't tell me! First I'll need to find eight white mice and a pumpkin!"

"Don't be so disagreeable. You might at least hear my idea, when I have been at such pains all afternoon to con it."

They were by now standing at the top of the set, awaiting the music, and Lord Markham was aware that their conversation was being viewed with speculative toleration by almost everyone in the ballroom. Sense told him that the sooner he and Miss Needwood could extricate themselves from these marriage rumors, the better it would be for both of them, especially after his sister's words. But he enjoyed Eleanor's company: She made him laugh. It seemed a pity not to keep their friendship. He agreed, with the expectation of considerable entertainment, to hear her new idea.

Knitting her brow, and looking absurdly like a child in a nursery, she revealed to him the ingredients of her plot. "I thought that this time we should try something uncomplicated," she explained kindly, again leaning toward him so as not to be overheard.

"Well, that's a relief, anyhow. I don't think I'm up to any more footpads."

"I still think you were rather fainthearted there," Eleanor admitted, sidetracked by the memory of her favorite firstborn idea. "A little more fortitude, and we might well have carried the day."

"Let us admit straightaway that I am lily-livered and get on to plan number two, else our dance will be over."

Eleanor did not answer him immediately, for the dance having just begun, Lord Markham had taken both her hands into his for the first time, which left her feeling suddenly rather shy, though she managed to answer him some few seconds later with much her usual composure and a good deal of absurdity. "Not lily-livered, but you *are* a bit of a sober-sides, you know, so I am being especially careful not to worry you at all. What do you think of a lover's quarrel? Nobody could take exception to our calling off our betrothal for such an everyday reason. And if we are *seen* to quarrel, there will be no question of people saying that *one* of us has simply cried off! I've given it a great deal of consideration, and it seems to me to be just the thing. And at Almack's, which I thought much the best place."

"Almack's!" The very hair on the back of his neck stood erect in horror. "My dear girl! You are surely not really thinking of causing a scene at Almack's?"

"Why not? It need not be *much* of a scene. Just a little head-tossing and prancing off the floor. Just to let people see that neither of us likes the other very much. At Almack's nobody will suspect that it is not a real quarrel, for who would dare such a thing in that holy place? It is an excellent notion, isn't it? I'm only surprised I didn't think of it before."

Lord Markham paled. "Do you know what would happen to us if we caused a scandal at one of Lady Jersey's assemblies?"

Eleanor declared that she really hadn't given it much thought.

"I rather think that you have *not*! No vouchers! Only think how you'd like that. And probably not just for you and me, but even my sister, and my poor innocent mama. I pray, if you have any fellow feeling for me at all, leave Almack's out of it. Even Mama would have me disinherited if I caused a scene there! Sally Jersey is one of Mama's best friends, you know, and would like nothing more than to have to endure the misery of being unable to send her vouchers!"

Miss Needwood was forced to see the sense in what he said and promised to try again, trusting him to keep up his spirits, since she really was sure that it could be only a matter of time before she hit on the very thing. She had no idea how very beautiful she looked, gazing up at him so earnestly, her blond head and bare shoulders rising up out of a billow of white silk. Lord Markham wondered briefly if there was any insanity in his family, for surely most men would suspect him of it if they heard him making plans to try to wriggle out of a betrothal with such a lovely creature. His sister's words floated at the back of his mind, and he reflected idly on the fact that most of his acquaintances must be expecting to hear of his marriage plans any day now. He had a fleeting disconcerting thought that life with Eleanor might be quite as delightful as it would be unpredictable, a thought he deliberately suppressed, thinking ruefully that the sooner they thought up a really useful plan to make him a free man, the safer he would be from the insinuating domestic picture that had begun to threaten him so dangerously. He wondered briefly if Cecily had told Eleanor that even his parents wanted them to marry, then shook his head. She'd never have been able to keep something like that to herself.

It was perhaps fortunate that Mr. Francis Hervey chose that precise moment to thread his way through the crowd on the floor toward them. Though he could

99

have whirled Eleanor away before Francis reached them and kept her to himself, his sporting instinct led him to take her out of the dance to introduce them.

"I would have known you anywhere, Miss Needwood," said the gallant Francis, bowing over her hand. "The description circulated of you was, for once, quite extraordinarily apt."

"My description? Why, what do they say?"

"Only that you are by far the most beautiful girl in town, what else? I should have known you at once, though I had nobody to introduce us."

Eleanor, still too new to town society to be quite at ease under such a compliment, blushed delightfully.

"Your friend is a flatterer, sir," she said, turning to Lord Markham. "You should have warned me."

"Hervey is known for it, aren't you, Francis? He has told every girl from here to Newcastle that she is the prettiest girl in England, so I wouldn't take too much notice of him if I were you."

He did not realize until Eleanor threw him a frosty glare how ungallant his words sounded. "No, I won't, sir!" she assured him coolly. "How good of you to warn me that Mr. Hervey must certainly be mistaken when he calls me beautiful!"

Flustered, Lord Markham disclaimed with annoyance while Francis laughed at his discomfort.

"Markham has always had a silver tongue, Miss Needwood," Francis told Eleanor. "I don't know why you waste your time on such a paltry fellow. But *I'm* in town now, so you need trouble with him no longer. And I suppose the clumsy oaf has been hauling you about with him all over the ballroom, too! Fellow can't dance a step! Never could!"

"I seem to remember that we had the same dancing master," said Markham, recovering himself adroitly. "So you may as well continue to have your toes stepped on by me, Miss Needwood, as let Hervey walk all over them. My sister says he just about passes muster in a ballroom as long as he remembers to bring with him his pocket book of steps. Otherwise he can't find his way through a country dance, let alone a cotillion!"

"Not true, ma'am. As I can prove to you at once, if Markham will only give you up to me for the rest of this dance."

"Not a chance, dear boy," said Markham, taking Eleanor's hand and placing it firmly on his arm before she had a chance to protest. "Miss Needwood is promised to me for the full half hour, and I'm dashed if I'll let you steal her from me."

"There'll be other dances, Miss Needwood," said Francis, unabashed. "And rest assured I'll not be behindhand in claiming you for them. Indeed, I trust that while I'm in town you will allow me the honor of escorting you? I'm here for my sister's come-out, so I shall need you to be very kind to me."

Without giving Eleanor a chance to reply, Markham led her back into the set, out of the reach of Francis's scheming.

Markham noticed a chill in Eleanor's demeanor, and when the dance brought them together, he murmured under his breath, "You know you really *must* speak to me, Miss Needwood, or we'll find ourselves in the middle of that lovers' quarrel we've been trying to avoid. You know that we'd agreed that that plan wouldn't do."

"Only at Almack's!"

"Not anywhere, if it's all the same to you. I know

you don't want to marry me, but it would be too bad of you not to wish to remain friends with me after all I've been through on your behalf. I must tell you that I've already ruined my reputation with my brother-in-law by admitting that I let you take me to Bullock's this morning, and if you only don't frown at me so, I may yet let you drag me along to the Italian opera—though I must confess that I may not quite manage to summon up sufficient courage to sit through it all."

She gazed up at him innocently. "But surely, sir, you won't wish to be seen in such commonplace company as mine?"

"Yes, that was very bad of me, wasn't it? Hervey always could tie me up in knots when he put his mind to it. Not that you *really* suspect me of considering you commonplace, so don't pretend you do. Whatever other men may think, I at least have already admitted I find your face the loveliest I've seen. I told you so at Bullock's. And I can bring forward at least one zebra and several snakes who can vouch for it."

"Ah, but you were practicing, sir, don't you remember?"

"Then I must have learned my lesson very quickly, mustn't I? I am quite perfect in it now."

His serious tone made her think that she must have misheard him, and she looked up at him inquiringly. His face told her that she had heard him perfectly, and she looked away, hoping that he would not see how he had brought the blood rushing up to her neck and face. Her father's warning that she should avoid getting herself into a scrape resounded in her mind, and she wondered with a failing heart if she was busy doing just that. She was not yet ready to admit, even to herself, the importance Lord Markham was assuming in her life, but she was forced, at least, to acknowledge that she had begun to find him disconcertingly agreeable, and to experience a seductive comfort in sharing her time with someone who shared her sense of humor. Was that what "harmonious to the spirit" meant? She resolved to guard herself in the future, and said lightly, "Well, sir, you are not to boast, for I have at least one other person whose devotion I have no reason to doubt. Mr. Fairfax, you know, is still pleading with me to sit for my portrait."

"Then he obviously has more taste in ladies than in clothes. But you are not telling me that you are really going to let him paint you? You'd be better spending your time with Hervey than that paltry fellow."

"Your sister thinks I should, but I doubt if I have the patience to sit still for so long. He speaks of five sessions! My papa would say I could not sit still for five minutes!"

"Excellent. Your papa must certainly be allowed to be the best judge of what would suit you. And only think to what better purpose you might put those five mornings. Why, we might go driving in St. James's Park, or for a saunter around Kew, and that even before you search in your guidebook for more museums."

Eleanor didn't answer him, still trying to decide whether prudence demanded that she see less, not more of him. After all, hadn't he made it perfectly clear that the rumor of their betrothal had been the last thing in the world he wished to hear?

"Well, Miss Needwood," said Markham more urgently, for he had just caught sight of Mr. Hervey's head above the crowd to remind him that if he did not secure Eleanor's company, others would. "Tell me that

I may take you for a drive in my curricle tomorrow. You shall see the guards parade and listen to the band. What say you?"

"I suppose I must say yes, sir, of course," said Eleanor, having won the battle against her good intentions. "Our public expects it. And yes, St. James's will be delightful. Shall you ask Cecy, too?"

"In a curricle, Miss Needwood? How can I?" He managed to look regretful, though his eyes were dancing. "I am afraid it must be just the two of us."

"Oh, what a pity," she replied, her eyes as bright as his.

Eleanor was, on the whole, relieved that Veren refused to be deprived of the dance he had stolen from Lord Markham, thinking that she had shown Markham favor enough for one evening, and went off with him to take her place in the dance and enjoy a satisfactory flirtation.

Hervey, meanwhile, was dancing with Cecily, not much to either's satisfaction: Hervey had his eyes fixed on Miss Needwood and was grinding his teeth in helpless impotence: Cecily, not used to being neglected by Mr. Hervey, with whom she had had in the past several satisfactory flirtations, looked on, becoming gradually more indignant.

"How pleasant it is to dance with old friends," she began at last after waiting in vain for him to remember her presence. "So restful not to be obliged to dress up one's conversation."

When he didn't answer, she tried again, very patiently for her. "I said, Francis, how restful it is not to have to *talk*."

He glanced down at her and then back almost at once to Eleanor, saying only, "Mmm . . ."

Much as Cecily admired Eleanor herself, this was not to be borne. In vexation, she stood still on the ballroom floor and stamped her foot in its satin slipper. "Francis Hervey, if you don't talk to me this moment, I shall . . . I shall never speak to you again."

"Sorry, Cec," said Francis ruefully, rubbing his chin. "Lost myself for a minute."

She followed his glance, which had once again turned toward Eleanor. "Don't lose yourself there, Francis," she said complacently. "I fully expect her to marry Markham, you know."

"As a matter of fact, I did hear something to that end, but Markham told me himself there's nothing in it!"

"Yes, isn't he droll," said Cecy, not the least ruffled, for she had already heard as much from Hartley. "But then, he was almost bound to say that, I suppose, until he has put it to the test." She leaned a little closer to him and whispered conspiratorially, "Between you and me, Francis, even Mama likes the match."

"Oh, I see! You and your ma like the match, so poor old Markham is to be dragged kicking and screaming to the altar! You women!"

"Not a bit of it, Francis," replied Cecily indignantly. "I have very good reasons for thinking Markham will propose . . . eventually."

"Just because you get him to propose—if you get him to propose—doesn't mean he'll be accepted."

"Not accepted? Rot!"

"Not everyone thinks your brother irresistible. There are other people who could give him a run for his money. Veren, for example. Or me. She really is the most delicious girl. Quite the most beautiful in the room."

"Oh, thank you," said Cecily in a burst of indignation. "What an entrancing partner you are. How dear of you to be so complimentary to your partner about another woman."

"Now, don't pretend to be so strung up, Cec," said Francis shrewdly. "You don't want me. Never did. I wore my heart on my sleeve long enough for you, but it was a different Hart you wanted."

Cecily's mouth curved in contentment. "Oh, there's nobody like Hart," she said, smiling a secretive little smile, "but you are not to spoil things between Markham and Miss Needwood."

There was a contented feeling in Eleanor's breast as she took her place in Lady Cecily's coach in the small hours, and she listened to her chatter about the ball with only half an ear while her memory floated her once more through her dance with Lord Markham.

There were just the two of them in the coach. Hartley had gone on to Brooks's with some friends, leaving Eleanor to listen to the monologue with which Cecily regaled her on the journey home. Still in her dreamworld, Eleanor was only vaguely aware of Lady Cecily's clever tongue as it passed over the evening's guests, dropping lightly as a butterfly on each, just long enough for an irreverent word or wickedly accurate description.

"Don't you agree that one could carry fashion too far? Surely someone should drop the merest hint to Madame de Lieven that that dreadful turban sits ill on her! It accentuates her neck, I'm sure it does. And yellow, too, which quite reminds one of a custard served on a stemmed dish," and "Did you hear the new duchess venting her spleen, poor thing, at how badly she is being treated by the queen, and only because she has been divorced before her marriage to Cumberland? Trust the dear queen not to lower *her* standards!" and "I had it in the strictest confidence from De Lieven that it is perfectly true that Castlereagh *was* hooted and pelted when he went to the hustings for Maxwell. It must have been dreadful! How I should have laughed to have seen it, so proper as he is!"

Eleanor was rather tired after the ball, but had an overwhelming wish to speak of Lord Markham. Not wanting to bring up his name directly, she first mentioned his friend Mr. Hervey.

"Oh, he is a sad rattle," said Cecily sharply. "I shouldn't take any notice of anything *he* says."

"How very lowering," said Eleanor with a low chuckle. "Mr. Hervey told me I was the most beautiful girl in town, and you are the second person since who has told me not to believe him."

"Who else told you?"

"Your brother."

"Markham? That was not very well done of him. And yet, you know, I by no means despair of *him* coming up to scratch."

"Coming up to scratch? With whom?"

"Why, with you, of course."

"But you know that is all nonsense," said Eleanor a trifle testily.

Cecily took a deep breath, determined to be candid. "You may as well know, my love, that I have quite made up my mind that you will be my sister."

"Cecily! You must not even think such a thing," she protested, though there was a warm feeling spreading through her at the thought. Maybe Markham had said something to Cecily that made her think he liked her!

"But it's true. I do want you for a sister. And so I told Markham while we were watching you with Fairfax."

"You *told* Markham," said Eleanor in a hollow voice.

"Of course. I thought it could not hurt. Indeed, I said that he could not choose anybody who would please me more."

"But he has no *intention* of marrying me. He never had."

"Very likely not. But people think he has, which I did just remind him. There is nothing like a little pressure to make a man do the right thing. And once he gets an idea in his mind, well . . ."

"Cecily! That's blackmail! How could you," cried Eleanor, the warm, pleasant feeling turning suddenly to heat across her face and neck. "You have spoiled everything. What did he say?"

"He didn't say much, but he did look thoughtful, which is a good sign. And I told him that Mama likes you, too!"

"You told him! How unfair of you." She broke off, quite unable to continue, and stared out the window into the night, unseeing. Her head was in a turmoil. That Cecily should have said such a thing to her brother! Should have put him in such a position! Should have put *her* in such a position! For a few moments she was quite at a loss as to what to say or do, so upset was she. Now she would never know if he liked her for herself. She felt tears spring to her eyes and blinked them back. Taking a deep breath, she turned her face back into the coach. "Now, listen," she said firmly, grabbing Cecily's hand and squeezing it firmly. "You must understand something at once. I don't *want* to marry your brother! I should not marry him if he asked me. The difference in our stations precludes it. And besides, I just don't!"

"That's silly! Nobody could prefer Sir Maltby to my brother!"

"I don't intend to marry him, either," said Eleanor hotly. "It may interest you to know that there are *other* men in the world!"

"Oh, a herd of them. But getting them to the altar is something else," said Cecily, refusing to be rattled. "So it can't hurt to widen your options. You take it too seriously."

"I don't," said Eleanor, attempting to laugh, for the last thing she wanted was to let Cecily see how mention of her brother had distressed her. "But you are not to try to bludgeon your brother into marrying me!"

"As if I would. I merely mentioned to him—merely reminded him, as it were—that people expected him to marry you and that he really owed it to you to do so! I don't see how that could hurt, since he knew it already."

"Cecily!"

"And what about the succession? He's nearly thirty. He has to be married soon."

Eleanor realized the futility of trying to make Cecily act more responsibly and decided instead to pretend to take it just as carelessly. "Well, you might reassure him, dearest, that even if others may have caught the wrong end of the stick, I have not. Certainly if everyone else expects him to marry me, I, at least, would be very surprised by it, since I should certainly refuse him if he asked me, thirty or not. Just tell him he is too *old* for me."

CHAPTER

11

And was that *his reason for being so attentive last night?* brooded Eleanor the next morning as she sat up in her bed against the pillows, picking at her breakfast. *His mother likes me, his father likes me, his sister says he must marry me because everyone expects it, so he does as he is told. What an idiot! "I find your face the loveliest I've seen, Miss Needwood." "Let me take you to the park, Miss Needwood." I thought he was being unusually attentive. Why has he done this when we had been such good friends? Has he all the time thought me as much a title hunter as all the other women he knows? Does he actually think that I am out to trap him? And worse! Is he so idle that as long as his parents like me, he is willing to play along?*

Her brows snapped together, then relaxed into their neat crescents. *No, that can't be so. He will be as vexed with Cecily as I am, for a certainty, but he will know that I have not encouraged her. Indeed, he is sure to tell me all about it today and know that I must be just as cross as he.* They would be as good friends as ever. And they would plan everything together as before. Nothing need change between them. She jumped out of bed impatiently, to choose her most becoming carriage dress.

I bet he can't wait to tell what Cecily said to him, she thought to herself with a smile as she rang for her water.

Meanwhile, Lord Markham, too, was indulging in heart searchings. Used as he was to living entirely to suit himself, he had become aware that his dealings had begun to get decidedly out of control. The news that his parents approved of Eleanor had shaken him to the core. His mother might wish to see him married to a respectable young woman, but that was Mama. A fond expression flitted briefly across his face as he thought of her. And if he could find a woman like her, maybe he *would* be tempted. But he'd seen too many friends caught in the parson's mousetrap with a shrew to wish to emulate them. His life suited him very well: indulging in his favorite sports, dipping into the lives of society ladies when the mood took him, and always adhering strictly to his rule not to raise expectations in maidenly bosoms. He had no desire to chase after any more regular union. His mother could nag him as much as she wished and so, for that matter, could his father (and here, his features hardened momentarily). Precious easy for *him* to prate on about a suitable connection. Only the saintliness of Mama's disposition made their marriage tolerable. Suppose he found himself married to someone with such an irascible temper as his father's. He wouldn't have the patience to deal with it. Let Gawaine marry and get the heir. He preferred the Lady Violets of the world. You knew where you were with them and could avoid the married state forever if you were lucky.

It was altogether surprising, then, that his association with Miss Needwood had found him so unprepared. As a prudent man, perhaps he should find a way of ridding himself of the sham of this betrothal as speedily as possible.

He shook his head and laughed, berating himself for taking the matter so seriously. She was only a girl, after all. What harm could a little flirtation do? Like an inept Odysseus failing to secure the knots while he had himself tied to the mast, Lord Markham comforted himself with the pretense that he was still master of the game, even as the horses to his curricle were being harnessed for him to take Miss Needwood to St. James's Park.

The dress Eleanor wore for the park, a round dress of lilac bombazine, was rather a plain affair after all, but she wore it because it provided the perfect foil to the exquisite bonnet that matched it. Of gray velour simulé lined with white sarcenet, a bunch of lilac silk flowers placed to one side of the crown, this delightful confection, with its wide lilac silk strings, was the prettiest of Eleanor's hats, and in it she appeared to Lord Markham, when he collected her from Grosvenor Square, the picture of loveliness.

For once she was not in a chattering sort of mood. Indeed, other than passing on punctiliously the regards to him received from her mama in a letter that morning, and informing him with enforced brightness that Mrs. Needwood hoped to be returning to town in a month now that Charlotte was so much better, and that they would then begin preparing for her presentation, she sat quite silent beside him, waiting for him to report to her what Cecily had said about them. Moments passed, then minutes, during which Lord Markham mentioned the balminess of the day, the certainty that the rain would hold off, and any amount of trivia from last night's ball, but not one word did he venture on the subject of Cecily! Or, indeed, of his parents! Her lips began to tighten, and by the time they had reached the park and they still had not been mentioned, she had to admit to herself that far from being her friend, he must think her a fortune hunter of the worst sort.

"You are very quiet, Miss Needwood," said Lord Markham eventually, when he noticed she wasn't answering him. "Are you busy making up more of your plots?"

"I certainly am," said Eleanor unequivocally. "It's beginning to be imperative that we do something to free ourselves from this tangle."

"Oh, not so imperative, surely," he said with a charming, intimate smile that at once quite took her breath away and made her indignant at the same time. He was actually flirting with her. How dare he flirt with her now that he thought she wished to marry him! She would show him that his addresses, far from being sought, were entirely unwelcome.

"Oh, I cannot agree with you there, sir," she said, looking serious. "I think we cannot loose ourselves from this tangle too quickly. And I do have one or two ideas that might do the trick. The one I favor is by far the easiest to arrange."

"I cannot wait to hear it!"

And Eleanor, tingling for want of retaliation, could not wait to reveal it to him. Smiling sweetly, she said, "Well, sir, it seems to me that we must make you something of a martyr."

"A martyr? Hmm, I'm not sure I like the sound of that!"

Eleanor was annoyed with herself for having to fight the urge to giggle. "I'm sorry about that, sir, but it really isn't so very bad. And all we have to do to bring it about is to arrange for you to receive just the tiniest injury. Nothing much, but I'm afraid the effects will have to be permanent if they are to do at all. Perhaps a limp. I strongly favor a carriage accident as the easiest to set up, though you may think of something better. A fall from a small outbuilding or some such thing."

He screwed up his face fastidiously. "Must it be a limp? I think I would find it difficult to limp about forever."

"Not a limp, then. In that case we might make it an ulcerated sore that doesn't heal, if you prefer, though that is more difficult, naturally."

"An ulcerated sore? While I hate to cavil at such a mere piece of inconvenience, Miss Needwood, how will it help us?"

"It means, silly, that you can refuse to let me sacrifice myself on the altar of matrimony, as Mama would say. You will know how to put it, won't you, for *you are such a good actor*. You will never be a whole man. Conscience will not allow you to entice a lovely young girl, etc. And no one could possibly blame me if you refuse to marry me, could they?"

"But nobody else will wish to marry me, either."

"I thought you did not want to marry, sir. Aren't all our efforts *supposed* to be taking us in that direction?"

"That's not to say that I won't ever want to marry. And how can I ask someone else if I've told everyone I never will?"

She sighed. "So you do not like that plan, either. How difficult you are. One would think that you did not wish to be released from our connection, had not one been *assured* that you did. The other plan is not nearly so easy to arrange."

He fidgeted uncomfortably. "Tell me about it."

"Well, if you are sure. Only I haven't finished off the details yet. I've been toying with the idea of perhaps having you suspected of stealing, oh, some little thing or other, and sent to a penal colony in Australia, though, as I say, the planning is still in its early stages."

His eyes and mouth looked startled for a moment, then hardened into suspicion. "Tell me, Miss Needwood, have I offended you at all?"

"What, you? How can you ask, Lord Markham?" She looked up at him, smiling seraphically, and then away into the distance, leaving him with a feeling that she bore him a distinct grudge.

Feeling not at all comfortable, he was just then turning his curricle onto the gravel path leading to the parkland in St. James's, where the guards paraded. There were already some dozen or so carriages pulled up by the side of the field, and Markham drew his neatly in behind them, intending when he had done so to try to find out what had upset his companion. He had just tossed his reins to his groom, when Eleanor cried out in a voice that suggested that the world could offer no greater felicity, "Oh, look, sir! There's Mr. Fairfax. Two or three carriages ahead. And he is sketching, too. What luck!"

Lord Markham's eyes followed hers, hoping she had been mistaken, but Fairfax was there all right—floppy bow, long hair, Cossacks, and all, leaning rather too

116

nonchalantly against his carriage, resting a sketching pad on his forearm while he crayoned industriously.

Markham cursed under his breath, while for Eleanor it was the answer to a prayer. If Markham thought he had only to drop the handkerchief for her to pick it up, it would become her mission in life to prove him wrong.

"Do you think we might pretend we have not seen him and walk off in the other direction?" said Markham hopefully.

"Why should we wish to? I shall be able to see his drawings at last, which Lady Cecily requires me most particularly to do."

"Does it have to be today?"

"I may never get another opportunity."

"I doubt that. The gods are not usually so kind."

"It is too late now, anyway, for he has seen us. See, he is waving."

"There is not the least need to wave back. We can still escape."

"Come, sir," she said, taking him by the arm. "Let us go over and see what view he had chosen to draw. He seems happy to see us, at all events. Only see, he is coming this way to meet us."

And indeed he was, and with a heightened color to his cheek and a complaisant look in his eye, which suggested to Markham that he was not altogether displeased to be found in such an artistic pose. Eleanor would really have liked to kick him for looking like such an affected ass, but that wouldn't help her at all in the small matter of denting Lord Markham's self-esteem. Instead, she held out her hand to him in the friendliest manner.

"I say, Miss Needwood, is it really you?" he said as if he could not believe his luck. "I was thinking of you, and there you were. I call that something indeed. Preordained."

"Yes, and I ordained it," said Lord Markham heavily. "You heard Miss Needwood telling my sister last night that we were to come to see the parade this morning."

"*Did* you say you were coming? I can't say I heard you," said Mr. Fairfax with scant regard for truth. "But now that you are here . . ."

"Now that I am here, Mr. Fairfax, won't you show me your sketch?" asked Eleanor. "I know so few artists that it will be a delight to me."

He showed just enough reluctance before agreeing to allow her to see what he described as his "simple little sketch. Just the veriest outline, and the rest to be done in the studio. Most artists fill in more detail, but I find I need only the odd line here and there to remind me of a scene."

Eleanor knew enough of drawing to be disappointed. It was schoolboy stuff, and Lord Markham, looking over her shoulder, did not hesitate to snort his contempt. "Odd lines, indeed!" he muttered, sotto voce.

Eleanor was quick to drown his lack of enthusiasm in an excess of praise. Her opinion of Orlando's talent exactly matched Lord Markham's, but it did not suit her to admit it. She held the little drawing as if entranced. "Really, Mr. Fairfax, it almost tempts me to sit for you if you still want me."

Could the issue be in doubt? Does the starving mongrel refuse a bone? In a few moments, and to Lord Markham's complete disgust, Eleanor had settled matters in a manner highly satisfactory to herself. The question of when she was to sit was all that remained to be decided. Mr. Fairfax, tentatively suggesting the following day, was only the more delighted when Eleanor expressed her impatience to see his studio without delay. Would it be shameless to ask him to take her now? She noticed that he had his mama's barouche, which would give them ample room for Lady Cecily. Couldn't they collect her on the way, for she knew how much dearest Cecy wished her to sit for her portrait for Mr. Fairfax.

Without knowing how she had managed it, Lord Markham found himself shaking hands with Miss Needwood, saw her led away to Orlando's carriage, and climb in, and watched Orlando whip up his horses, Miss Needwood turning back to wave at him with the cheeriest wave and an air that suggested that it was some sort of consolation prize. He stood looking after them, rubbing the lobe of his ear. *Now* what had that girl got into her head?

CHAPTER

12

Picture an artist's studio: an attic at the top of a dark, crumbling stairway in a dank, dingy house.

Mr. Fairfax's studio was not like that at all. Indeed, Miss Needwood was sure they must have come to the wrong place, until Lady Cecily whispered that it was perfectly true that Mr. Fairfax's studio really did form part of his mama's own handsome Mayfair mansion. So much for impoverished artists, for it was clearly not in Mr. Fairfax's scheme of things to share the hardship even if he hoped to share the glory. No attic for him: His studio was seen at once to be a spacious, airy apartment with splendid plasterwork ceilings, walls of delicate pale blue wash, expensive marble floors, and drapes of velvet to match the furniture coverings. A striped sofa sat next to a bureau bookcase filled with books of art prints, to one side of which was placed an artist's table. Dotted about were the odds and ends of furniture one might expect to find in any gentleman's residence, but by far the most notable objects in the studio were Mr. Fairfax's magnificent easel and a dais supporting the royal-blue-satin-covered throne used by his models.

The three of them, Orlando, Eleanor, and Cecily, had

arrived some time before and had just finished inspecting some of Mr. Fairfax's paintings before deciding on a pose for Eleanor, when a flurry of activity from out in the hallway heralded the arrival of his mama. Out shopping in Bond Street, she had clearly not expected to be receiving visitors on her return. Some low-toned, agitated conversation with the footman took place outside the door, after which it opened onto a mild-looking elderly little lady who wandered in without a word and looked all about her in the manner of a harried dormouse.

Dressed in a black-beaded smock and trailing a purple shawl, Mrs. Fairfax wore no cap, her hair, which was frizzy and of an aptly mouselike hue, being held in a bandeau tied low on her forehead, from which Miss Needwood deduced that it was from his mama that Mr. Fairfax must have inherited his artistic tendency. She could not have been more wrong: Mrs. Fairfax hadn't a scrap of the artist in her. In fact, it would have been difficult to point to any accomplishment she could claim as her own. But since she had begun to fancy her son an artist, she had felt that she owed it to him, somehow, to look the part of his mother.

She came in, looking surprised to see them though the butler had clearly told her they were there, moving toward Orlando as if for refuge.

"Ah, there you are, dearest," she said anxiously. "You did not get wet in the park?"

"How could I, Mama? It is not raining outside. You remember, we spoke about it before you went out."

"Oh, no, that's right. Not raining. No more it is! Well, how fortunate. It wasn't raining in Bond Street, either. And Dassett tells me we have visitors. Did we know they were coming, dear? There's no cake, you know. My at-home is not until Friday, and you never eat it. No cake at all. I told cook she might have the last of the seed cake yesterday, for *we* never like it, do we? And besides, it was beginning to be a little stale. I can see if she has eaten it if you wish?"

Mr. Fairfax threw his visitors an agonized glance and pulled his mama to one side of the room out of earshot. In a voice meant only for her, he said, "It's all right, Mama. Lady Cecily and Miss Needwood weren't expecting anything. Just some tea. Miss Needwood has agreed to sit for me and wanted to see the studio."

"What's that, my boy?" asked Mrs. Fairfax in the loud tones of the hard of hearing. "Won't want anything? Only tea, did you say? Speak up, dear, so I can hear you."

With a desperate glance toward the ladies, who were studiously pretending not to listen, he hissed, "Where's your ear trumpet, Mama? Where have you put it down?"

"Crumpets, dear? I'm sorry. Cook makes those only during winter. If you'd said you wanted them . . ."

"I said, where's your ear trumpet?" he shouted, but seeing only a blank expression, he gave it up. "Come and be introduced properly, Mama," he said in a very loud voice. "Lady Cecily you know already, don't you?"

"Lady Cecily? Of course I know Lady Cecily, Orlando. There's no need to shout! How are you, my dear? But I need not ask, for you look blooming. Quite the image of your poor dear mama when she was your age. Though, now I come to think of it, wasn't she a good deal darker? How is the poor thing? Dropsy! Such a curse! I suppose they have her on laudanum?"

"Dropsy? My dear ma'am, Mama doesn't have dropsy. She is in perfect health," said Lady Cecily, now quite as bewildered as her hostess.

"Is she now? Isn't that wonderful! I suppose it is Knighton has done it? What a marvelous physician he is!"

"But Mama has never *been* ill. Oh—I think I see. Might you be thinking of Lady Melbourne, Mrs. Fairfax? *My* mama is Lady Fildes. I'm Lady Cecily Fienne, you know."

The elderly lady peered at her intently. "So you are! How silly of me! I thought you were not dark enough for one of Eliza Melbourne's daughters. She was always so—"

"And here is Miss Needwood, Mama," said her son, breaking ruthlessly in. "She is wanting to be introduced to you."

Now, that was a name Mrs. Fairfax could *not* mistake. She had heard nothing but "Miss Needwood" from her son's lips for weeks, and she went forward eagerly, with her hand outstretched. Orlando's doting mother she might be, but she was not possessive and wished above all to help him achieve his every desire. If Miss Needwood was one of those desires, it should not be through any omission of *hers* if Orlando did not win her. Miss Needwood's family (though, to be sure, she had never heard of them!) must be respectable, else she would not be staying with Lady Cecily. As for fortune, her darling Orlando, praise be, need not concern himself with anything so sordid.

"Miss Needwood, what a joy to meet you at last.

And so very pretty. Orlando and I don't always agree on—but nobody could possibly— Some tea, Miss Needwood? Lady Cecily? Let me have some tea brought. Orlando, ring the bell. Or chocolate, perhaps? Far too rich for me, but some ladies do? Ah, Dassett!" The door opened to reveal one of Mrs. Fairfax's liveried footmen and she went on. "Some tea, if you please. And some cake. Oh, no! No cake. But there are some macaroons. Stay! I gave the last of those to— Well now, how cozy we all are— Just move that shawl if it is in your way, Miss Needwood. I wondered where I had left— And such pretty hair as you have. No wonder Orlando wants to paint you."

"We were just deciding on a pose as you came in, Mama," said Orlando in some desperation. "Lady Cecily favors a full-length portrait, as I do. What do you think?"

"Full-length? Oh, yes, that would be delightful, though she *would* look beautiful seated. And the royal blue satin would set off her— But certainly, one or the other! You could not do better than to choose one or the other."

Lady Cecily bit her lip and tried not to catch Eleanor's eye as Mr. Fairfax's face took on a tortured expression. "Why don't you see what is keeping the tea tray, Mama, while we consider," he suggested, pulling nervously at his collar.

"What, dear? Paint her seated at the tea tray? If you think it will answer. Myself, I'd have thought—but you know best, I'm sure."

His mind torn between revulsion at the thought of painting Miss Needwood in such a commonplace pose and impatience with his mama, Mr. Fairfax clutched at his flowing locks. He spoke loudly to his mother, mouthing his words with precision.

"The tea tray, Mama. Go and find out what is keeping it, will you?"

Her affability quite unimpaired, the little lady rose at once to obey him.

"You will excuse me, won't you, Lady Cecily?" Then, leaning closer, she whispered confidentially, "My son wishes me to check on the tea tray, you know. And when my footman brings it, we shall see if the pose suits Miss Needwood."

As soon as the door had closed behind her, Mr. Fairfax turned back to his guests, explaining as calmly as he could, "Mama is sometimes confused. She is a trifle hard of hearing."

"I think she's a dear, Mr. Fairfax. One rarely meets with such unaffected goodwill nowadays."

He was quick to agree. If Miss Needwood didn't mind Mama, who was he to do so? He hastily returned to the problem occupying them, a problem so difficult to solve that by the time Mrs. Fairfax was coming back into the studio, the footman in her wake carrying a large silver tea tray, they had still not entirely decided between a portrait of Eleanor in morning gown, reclining on the sofa, and one in Grecian garb, against a background of pale silk draperies and with one arm resting on a marble pillar, the other clasping a shawl that would fall in folds to the floor.

"Don't mind me," Mrs. Fairfax said cheerfully, sending her son a loving smile. "I am here only to see that you have everything you need. I shan't disturb you. It's just my embroidery. I feel sure I left it— Oh, there it is— No, that is your paint rag. Shall I pour? Such a

125

heavy teapot! Oh, Lady Cecily, how kind. With my rheumatics, I find it so— No, I won't join you, if you will excuse me. I know you art lovers like not to be disturbed. Just pretend I'm not here. I shall be as quiet as a— Oh, there it is. Just when I thought I— No! Not my embroidery at all. How silly of me. That is the drapery you used when you painted Lady Violet, Orlando. Have you shown Lady Cecily and Miss Needwood your painting of dear Lady Violet? No? Oh, really you must, for it is quite one of your best. So unaccountable that she chose not to take it after all."

As she spoke, she moved some canvases stacked against the wall to reveal a gilt-framed portrait of a female. Eleanor was pleased that Mrs. Fairfax had given them a broad hint as to the sitter, for she would have had great difficulty in guessing that it was Lady Violet, a lady to be sure she did not know well but had seen sufficiently to at least be expected to recognize. She began to be glad that Mr. Fairfax had such an amusing mama, for certainly she could look forward to little other reward for the promised five sittings, if that single portrait was anything to go by.

As if guessing Miss Needwood's thoughts, Mr. Fairfax reddened and hunched his shoulder at his mama. "You remember, Mama, that we agreed that *that* portrait was *not* a success. I must take at least some of the blame, I suppose, but really, Miss Needwood, she *would* move every minute or so. There was no getting her to keep a pose at all. I think you'd be more pleased with the portrait I did of Lady Cowper. You may have seen it, for she has it hanging in her entrance hall? And there are one or two here that are not altogether to be despised. Pull out that one I painted of you, Mama. You will find it there, just by you."

Mrs. Fairfax, all in a fluster, moved three or four paintings without success in her search for the desired masterpiece, her movements punctuated by a very full description of her toils.

"Is it this one here? Oh, no, that is Alvanley— So good-natured! But then, I have known him forever. Such an agreeable— Orlando did not perfectly catch the eyes, I think, but really, a fine piece, so long as one remembers who it is supposed to— Now, is that it? No! That is the dear countess—De Lieven, of course, not one of *our* princesses, but quite a— Ah, what have we here? Just let me push this along—."

The last picture she moved was a large, heavily framed canvas, that, as she pushed it to one side, was shown to be disguising a cache of paintings. Probably neither Lady Cecily nor Eleanor would have taken much notice of them had not Mr. Fairfax let out an agonized groan and fixed his eyes on them in so much horror. As it was, they could hardly fail to notice that his vague mama had revealed, in all their glory, a dozen or so nudes. She, dear thing, had noticed nothing amiss, and took each one out in its turn in her search for the painting of herself, which her son had executed some time before, and which she suspected must therefore be at the very back. The paintings thus revealed proved to be all of ladies, rather statuesque ladies, reclining voluptuously at their ease on Mr. Fairfax's striped sofa. True he had painted the sofa in a number of guises: swathed in turquoise and pinks and greens: But its general shape was there for all to see, along with some accompanying hundredweights of female flesh. Had Mr.

Fairfax not been so mortified, Eleanor would have thought nothing of finding such paintings in an artist's studio, however poorly painted. But Mr. Fairfax's expression was so exactly reminiscent of a schoolboy caught stealing cakes from the pantry that she had to bite her cheek to prevent herself from laughing. Lady Cecily, who was at times inclined to be prudish, was not so amused: Such *warm* items might do for classical painters, for weren't the art galleries full of them? Though, to be sure, she had always wondered— They were, of course, entirely out of place in the studio of an amateur portrait painter. And especially a studio in his mama's house! She was hotly embarrassed and averted her eyes from the paintings as if the sight of them offended her.

In direct contrast, Mrs. Fairfax remained entirely unruffled. "I see you are looking at Orlando's portraits," she said complacently. "You are not to be shocked, Lady Cecily, for he has explained it all to me! What might be thought shocking in anybody else is quite permissible in an artist. One must needs study the unclothed female form," she recited as one well versed in the lesson, "in order to be better able to paint the clothed female."

"I do not see any male nudes, Mr. Fairfax. Does not the same principle apply to painting the male form?" asked Eleanor brightly.

Mrs. Fairfax seemed much struck by the thought. "I had never considered that, dearest," she said to him, exhibiting a vaguely puzzled demeanor. "Should not you be inviting some of the lower sorts of male persons to sit for you, my love? John Coachman would do, I think.

Did not you say that models were required to have the very fullest development? Or does that only apply to—"

"Well now!" intruded Lady Cecily brightly. "We simply *must* go, mustn't we, Nell? What a delightful morning we have had!"

Eleanor agreed at once, for she was finding it extremely difficult to exercise control over the hilarity that had been building up inside her all morning, and which this last threatened to release.

Mr. Fairfax looked at her anxiously. "You *will* come for your sitting tomorrow, Miss Needwood? And Lady Cecily, of course, to chaperone you?" This was said in such stolid tones, that had the equivocal paintings not still been clearly on show, they could have been forgiven for considering him the sternest guardian of propriety. As it was, it did indicate that Eleanor, at least, could be sure of no *warmer* treatment than was entirely permissible. She was glad of it, for she would not readily have given up her plans to show Lord Markham how well she could occupy herself without recourse to his protection.

Sending Mr. Fairfax a comfortable smile, she said without hesitation, "I shall look forward to it, Mr. Fairfax. And Lady Cecily will certainly come, too, won't you, Cecy? Only—*not* the sofa, I think. Shall we agree on the Grecian portrait?"

CHAPTER

13

Walking through the foyer of the opera house that same evening, Eleanor was surprised to see, bearing down on her, and in the full paraphernalia of evening dress, Lord Markham's well-proportioned form. He saw her, and the easy smile his face assumed deepened when she moved forward to meet him, hand outstretched: He could never resist her matter-of-fact good humor. Another woman would have simpered and made him come to her: Eleanor met him halfway.

She laughed up into his eyes, determined to be friendly, but no more than friendly. "My dear sir! Are you ill? Have they closed Limmer's Hotel? Is the Daffy Club quite broken up?"

He took her hand, tucking it into the crook of his arm, turning to walk with her toward the boxes. "A respectable girl knows nothing of such places, Miss Needwood."

She glanced sideways up at him with ill-concealed interest. "Are they, then, so very dreadful, sir? How I should adore to be allowed to see for myself."

"Well, don't say so to anyone else," he said hastily, pulling her to one side out of the flow of the crowd.

"Do you want to annihilate your reputation? And what are you doing walking about here alone?"

"Oh, I'm not afraid of my reputation. I've only been to pin some lace torn from my train: Your brother-in-law trod on it. I can hardly be hanged, drawn, and quartered for that. I am well versed in all your silly rules and am now on my way back to your sister like any well-brought-up girl. As for speaking of the Daffy Club, I should not *dream* of mentioning that to anyone else. *You* don't count."

"Thank you, Miss Needwood. I had almost forgotten the charm of your company, since I was so cavalierly denied it today."

"Don't be absurd," she replied, ignoring his criticism. "You know perfectly well what I mean. Mama expects me to find a husband, and unless I can find myself a sensible man, I fear I have to pretend to be as affected as all the other girls."

"That would be a pity."

"I think so, too," she said candidly, "but I can't help it if men are attracted to ninnyhammers."

"And Mr. Fairfax? What sort of girl attracts him?"

The question caught her unawares. She really didn't know how to answer it. She didn't mind using Mr. Fairfax to ruffle Markham's feathers, but she didn't want him to think she could really admire such a puppy. She prevaricated. "Oh, we don't start the sittings until tomorrow. I'll let you know then."

"I can't wait to hear!" There was a hint of steel in Markham's reply, which was irresistible to Eleanor's sense of humor.

"What a pity *you* did not immediately fall in love

with me, sir, for then I might have solved my problem," she said seriously.

An unnerving sensation overtook him at her words. For a moment he felt himself actually teetering on the edge of a proposal. Then he chanced to look down, and saw her face lit with amusement.

"I wish I might have caught your expression in a painting!" she giggled. "I have never seen anything so funny! Don't fear, I think I know better than to try for *you*. You'll *never* wed. It would be far too much trouble."

He noticed the firmness in her voice when she underlined that she wasn't going to try to get him, and was rather relieved. Ever since Cecily had reminded him that all of town expected them to marry, he had had a nagging fear that he might have been too friendly with Eleanor and perhaps she had expected it, too. Now that she had reassured him, he was glad to find himself back on firm ground, but her conception of his character could not help but pique him, especially after he had expended so much energy on her behalf.

"You still haven't told me why you are here," Eleanor reminded him. "You don't like the opera."

"Neither do you."

"But *I* am husband-hunting. Suppose I missed an opera-loving marquess, Mama would never forgive me. Does Veren like opera, do you think?"

He ignored what was plainly a leading question.

"I am here because I haven't been able to see you anywhere else," he said at last. "You did dump me rather unceremoniously this morning. And then, when I called in at Grosvenor Square after luncheon, you were out. I seemed to remember that you mentioned the opera. I knew Cecy uses my father's box, so I took a chance. I *thought* we were supposed to be pretending to be betrothed?"

"Ah, but that was *before*. When *we* thought people imagined us engaged," she reminded him. "But now I'm not so sure they ever *did*! The Marquess of Veren said *he* didn't believe it, even Mr. Hervey said that he thinks it all to be a hum! And he's one of your closest friends!"

"Francis? When have you seen him?"

"Oh, he was awaiting us when we returned from Mayfair," she said airily, "and he took me to meet his mama and his sister. What a delightful family they are, to be sure."

"He'd never do as a husband," he said at once.

"How so? Sure Mama would be in transports if I took him home as her son-in-law, for Cecy says his fortune is prodigious."

"So is his vanity!"

"Oh, I imagine I could deal with that!"

Markham felt his anger growing quite irrationally, until quite suddenly Eleanor's clear eyes met his.

"You've not the least intention of taking Francis, have you, wretch? Who is it has taken your fancy? Veren? Not that absurd artist fellow?" His cheeks ruddied, his grievance making him less cautious than usual. "I can't help wishing you hadn't decided to let him paint you."

She looked an enquiry.

"Well, you must know what an on-dit the ton will make of it. You might have thought of me before you let yourself be persuaded by that cawker. Whatever you may imagine, the town does still talk of us marrying.

They will conceive it the most delicious morsel that Lord Markham's betrothed cannot decide whether to take *him* after all or plump for a half-wit like Fairfax."

"Oh, no! And you such an ingenue that you won't know how to answer them."

There was a pause, and Eleanor looked up expectantly.

"You know, Miss Needwood, I think I understand why your mama wished to marry you off as speedily as possible. Indeed, I begin to think Sir Maltby a mile too good for you."

"Oh, I hope I can do better than that."

"If you're thinking of Veren, you'll catch cold," he said pleasantly.

"Oh? You don't think I've got much chance, then?" she said, keeping her face pleasant with much difficulty. "He was rather attentive last night."

"Seen him attentive to a dozen girls. Nothing in that."

She widened her eyes at him. "Really! Men are such *dears*, aren't they?"

"Women play the game just as much as men do," he reminded her.

"I'll bear that in mind, Lord Markham," she assured him with a humorous look. "So you don't think I'll get him to the opera, then?"

"Veren? Not a hope," he said, unaccountably annoyed by her insistence.

She smiled a secretive little smile, saying, "And I thought he liked me! Come, you shall take me back to your sister's box. And pray do stop glowering at me, else who will believe you adore me?"

"Adore you! That I do not!"

But when they reached Cecily's box, and he drew back the curtain for Eleanor to enter, an unwelcome surprise awaited him. His evening and his plans were spoiled. There, sitting on the edge of the box, was the Honorable Francis Hervey, looking quite at home, as if he had been there some time. And nearby, on one of the spindly opera chairs, was the Most Honorable the Marquess of Veren.

Francis grinned when they entered, and the viscount noticed he was wearing his satyr look.

"Ah, here you are at last, Miss Needwood," he began, as Eleanor lifted her skirts to step across the threshold. "I had begun to think I'd lost you, but I see you are only with Markham. Here, come sit by me."

"Yes, I met the girl outside, positively gasping for some good conversation," countered Markham, not at all pleased to see how readily Eleanor allowed herself to be led away, not by Francis, but by the marquess, who had kept a place for her at his side.

"And so you brought her back to me, *naturally*, dear old boy," said Veren. "How good of you."

"Had I *known* you were here, I'd have taken pity on her and found her a spot with more congenial company."

"Now, what a thing to say about your sister."

Markham acknowledged the hit with a grin, and taking a seat on the other side of Eleanor, he said, "I won't even dignify such a paltry thrust with an answer, Cecy. You will know how to deal with that!"

And indeed, Cecy knew quite well enough how to protect herself and her brother. Under cover of her vociferous indignation, Markham took an opportunity to deliver an invitation to Eleanor to go with him to an alfresco party the next day. To his chagrin, Lord Veren pointed out gently that she had already agreed to attend the party with *him*.

"You *have* been busy today, Miss Needwood," he said frostily. "No wonder you were so confident." And then to his sister, he added, "Your box is rather crowded, Cecily, I won't stay."

"Paltry fellow," said Francis gaily, "giving up so soon?"

"Oh, I was never one to just make up the numbers."

"Me, neither, Markham, old fellow," said Francis, touching his nose. "But I expect my turn to come later. Miss Needwood has promised to come to the Royal Circus with me to see an equestrian performance, don't you know."

"Busier and busier, Miss Needwood," said Markham with a touch of asperity. "I shan't stay."

"Oh, no! You *mustn't* go, Markham. There's plenty of room," wailed Cecily, indignant that he let the others win so easily.

Her brother kissed her cheek, but his eyes were on Eleanor. "Some, at least, of your party seem to have seen *quite* enough of me, sweeting," he remarked, and with a curt good-bye thrust in the midst of them all, he took his leave, with Francis's mocking laughter in his ears.

Depressed by his attitude, Eleanor stopped herself with the greatest effort of will from calling him back, but the evening, which had promised so well, had suddenly become sadly flat.

Markham dashed through the theater and down the stairway, eager to put as much distance as possible between himself and Eleanor. A group of people was making a late entrance into the foyer, but Markham's blood was up and he was all but past them, when Lady Pelham lightly touched his arm. Almost without realizing it, Markham had become one of her party and was seating himself beside her in her box, receiving her usual favors. Why should he have his evening ruined? While she was seating her guests where she wanted them, Markham borrowed Lady Violet's opera glass and looked about the theater. A number of acquaintances were variously packed into the auditorium, and many caught his eye to salute him. After Eleanor's indifference, it was pleasant to have so many female heads nodding to him encouragingly, and the world began to seem a better place. For a few minutes he was able almost entirely to forget Eleanor's transgressions—until, without thinking, he chanced to fix Violet's opera glass on his father's box. There, for the world to see, stood Veren and Miss Needwood rather apart from the others, very deep in what looked like a very *warm* conversation indeed. Certainly Eleanor was blushing. As though the couple felt his glass on them, they drew apart guiltily, and the next moment Veren, too, was looking around the auditorium, with rather too much unconcern. Markham, who imagined he had just witnessed a declaration, was too slow in drawing back into the shadow and suffered the extreme mortification of having himself pointed out to Eleanor.

Drat the girl! Now it would seem as if he was spying on them. And at such a time! Markham flushed to his hair roots. Without weighing up his actions, he pushed his chair close to Violet's and, without so much as a by-your-leave, lifted her hand to his lips, ensuring that they were now both well out of the shadows. However surprised, Lady Violet was not one to let opportunity pass her by. She fully encouraged Markham's flirting, glad to have him safely back in tow, and Eleanor was granted the exquisite annoyance of seeing the gentleman known to be her own cavalier showing an inexcusable degree of attention to another!

Eleanor had quite as much pride as Lord Markham, as that gentleman should be quick to learn. She tossed her head and set herself—in a warm show of affection to my lord Veren—to prove just how little Lord Markham's actions were of any interest to her.

And the fashionable world looked on in sheer delight as the two who had been tipped for the season's best match spent the entire evening proving just how mistaken society could be.

CHAPTER

14

Lady Cecily Fienne, opening her letters the following morning, was most sincerely annoyed when she reviewed the events of the previous evening. After all her work to promote the match between Eleanor and her brother—and when they had seemed to be getting on so well—it now seemed that they were hardly speaking to each other at all.

She opened another letter, found that it was a bill from Floris, the court perfumier in Jermyn Street, and dropped it onto a pile of others. Typical that just as the bills had begun to mount up again, her plans should start to go wrong.

Last night was disastrous! Never would she forget her mortification when they had chanced to run into that fearful Lady Pelham with her party in the foyer on leaving the opera house and Eleanor and Markham exchanged barely a nod. So obvious was their loathing of each other at that moment that even Hart had been moved to remind his wife to start saving up the twenty-five pounds to pay her debt now that her precious Markham had given up interest in Eleanor.

Oh, no! And now, to cap it all, here was a letter from her mama, asking whether the affair had moved forward. Moved forward! She'd like to see Mama moving such obstinate creatures forward. It was too provoking to see Eleanor throwing away her chance, when she had secured even Mama's approval. For if she thought she could get the marquess to come to the point, she had windmills in her head.

She had spoken quite sharply to Eleanor before they had retired to their own apartments, but had not been able to solicit from her the cause of the estrangement. All Eleanor would say was that she did not understand what all the fuss was about, since as far as she was concerned, Lord Markham was the merest acquaintance, which piece of nonsense had so enraged Cecily that they had ended up in a full quarrel. And now, instead of being able to make it up with her, she had been told by her maid that Miss Needwood had actually taken one of the footmen with her and had gone out early to return some books to Hatcham's. It was too maddening.

Pushing away her breakfast tray, she made the momentous decision to rise early and was just putting the finishing touches to her toilette, when Harrop announced her brother.

"Markham! Whatever brings you this early? Nothing's happened to Mama or Papa?"

"Good heavens, no!" Markham replied testily. "Why should it?"

"Well, it *is* only ten o'clock. You must admit, it isn't like you to be up and around so early."

"It isn't like you, either. I expected you to be still in bed. Where's Hart? I thought I'd join him riding. Has he had enough of you and run off to a monastery?"

"He's already gone. Ages ago."

Markham hesitated. "And Miss Needwood?"

"Eleanor is in a perfectly frightful mood and has gone out without me."

Lord Markham looked disappointed for a brief moment, but then brightened. "So it's just the two of us, then, Cec. I can't say I'm altogether sorry for the chance of a coze."

Lady Cecily became very busy at her dressing table, picking up a jeweled comb and fitting it high into the back of her hair.

"How hateful it is to have red hair," she said quickly, eager to prevent any deeper conversation. "It isn't fair that I should be so cursed while you and Gawaine escape it entirely. You and he don't have even a hint of red." She peered intently into the mirror, licking the end of her finger and running it over her eyebrows. "Thank heavens at least I haven't got sandy eyebrows and lashes."

"Funny thing, that. Seem to remember you had 'em as a girl," Markham reflected.

"Philip Markham!" cried his sister, springing to her feet in horror. "If you dare to tell anyone that I darken my eyebrows, I'll kill you! Even Hart doesn't know that I use elderberry lotion on them."

"Calm down, idiot. He shan't learn it from me. I don't want him sending you back. At least be grateful you haven't got freckles."

"But I don't take chances, for I've heard one can get them as one gets older. I always go to bed in Knighton's Lotion to keep them at bay."

"How happy for Hartley—but I didn't come to talk about beauty remedies." He paused suddenly, for he'd been idly letting his glance wander about the room.

"Here, just a moment, Cec. Haven't you changed this room?"

"No, I don't think so," she replied, slipping on her rings.

"But wasn't there a painting of the fourth earl on that wall?"

"Oh, that."

"And now that I think of it, didn't you have the two Lawrence portraits and those pretty miniatures over there? Where've you put them?"

"Don't you like the room better without them? So much lighter," she prevaricated.

"Oh, Cec! You haven't sold 'em? You can't keep selling everything! I told you to come to me when you need money. If I can't sub my own sister for a few years, I don't know what sort of brother I am."

"Dear Philip," she cried, running over and throwing her arms around him, "you are so sweet. And indeed, when you were so generous earlier this year, you did save that large battle scene in the salon from going the same way."

"Cecily! Father'll be furious if he finds out. If you overstretch yourself, apply to me. It is better than having all the family treasures put on the market—though Father deserves it with that ridiculous trust. If ever a woman needed her own money, you do, and it was stupid, once he'd agreed for you to marry Hart, not to give it to you. Now, don't ruin this neckcloth, little idiot. If you can't pay your bills, send 'em to me."

"But Hart won't let me," wailed Lady Cecily. "He's as bad as Father and says we should manage on his money."

"Hart is a good fellow, Cec, but if he wanted to manage on his fortune, he shouldn't have married the most prodigal woman in London. I trust you to persuade him. Remember, I don't expect to hear of any more sales."

"Darling, how sweet of you," said Cecily, then, thinking of Eleanor, she said vaguely, "I wish I'd known earlier that you were willing to . . ."

"Why? What've you done now?" he asked suspiciously.

But now that he'd made his promise and they were unnecessary, Cecily had no intention of telling him about her schemes in the matter of her brother and Miss Needwood. "Only that Mama scolded me miserably about selling the miniatures. Had I known earlier that you were prepared to help me out, she needn't have been upset."

"I won't *have* Mama made unhappy. Enough that she lives with that old termagant."

"But she *isn't* unhappy, Markham."

"Mama is a saint, but it can't be pleasant living with his temper."

Lady Cecily laughed her tinkling laugh. "But she *loves* him, Markham. And he loves her. She has him jumping through hoops when it pleases her. Just because you and Papa don't get on, you mustn't imagine Mama is miserable. Indeed, it has often seemed to me that with just a little push on your side, you and Papa might rub along very well. You should put Arno in order. You know how it would please him."

"Please him? He doesn't want me to please him: He wants me to *obey* him. You don't know the half of it. You were too young at the time. When I first inherited I was twenty—determined to do great things with it just to show Father that I wasn't the ninnyhammer he'd al-

143

ways made me feel. I read everything I could lay my hands on about new farming methods: took advice from, oh, any number of people, fool that I was. As if Father wanted that! He just wanted to tell me what to do and have me do it. That's why he persuaded me to take on Bates. So he could have a direct correspondent. I remember once—you will laugh—I read a treatise on land reclamation and it seemed just the thing for that marshy lower pasture. I was so enthusiastic, I couldn't wait to get started. This was my great chance to show him. I told Bates to put all in hand, but, as Father's *spy*, he naturally wrote at once. Without so much as a by-your-leave, Father told Bates to cancel my orders. Said that enough money had been wasted in the past on that piece of land. I should listen to 'older and wiser heads.' And it was like that whatever I did. I gave it up after about three years. If Father was giving Bates orders, I might as well leave it in his hands entirely."

"Why don't you get rid of Bates, Markham? I should if I had a dresser or a parlormaid who didn't obey my wishes. Hart says that Arno has the making of a very fine estate if you would only take things in hand."

"You and Hart *have* been thick with Miss Needwood, haven't you?" Markham replied grimly. "And speaking of Miss Needwood, I still haven't been able to find how that dashed rumor started."

"Yes, indeed. *Isn't* it irksome," she said sympathetically.

"Irksome! It's a darned sight more than that! I can tell you, it gave me a turn when I saw those bets in the book at Brooks's. I can't think how it started up. I wish you hadn't asked her to stay with you."

"Well, of all the ingrates!" cried Cecy indignantly.

"When her mama said that Nell must go home with her, what else could I do but ask her to stay, when you had expressly asked me to do what I could for her. Eleanor is a dear, but it is not easy having a guest for so long, Markham," she went on, lying without a qualm. "I did it only for you."

"I'm sorry, Cec. Of course you did. Whom do *you* suspect of spreading this rumor?"

"Naturally I have given it an inordinate amount of thought," replied Cecily with a huge sigh, not hesitating to perjure herself further. "I can't help wondering if it wasn't poor Nell's stepmama did it."

It was an excellent inspiration. Markham had no difficulty whatever in believing anything of that woman.

"Of course we shall never find out for certain," said Cecily with another great sigh. "But one thing I am absolutely certain of, it was not Eleanor. Why, when Mama and Papa came to town and she heard they had come to look her over, she was mortified."

"Yes, and that was something else. What made them come just when you had Miss Needwood here? You know Papa never comes to town in the season."

"Now, there I can help you, love," Cecy replied happily. "Lady Jersey wrote to Mama. I tell you, Markham, it gave me quite a turn when they said they were coming."

"Lord, yes, it must have. Poor Miss Needwood. I bet he gave her one of his rare dressing-downs!"

"Oh, no. I told you, he liked her," said Cecily airily. "Of course, once Mama decided that *she* liked Nell, it was only a matter of time before Papa was persuaded to it. And Mama was delighted with Nell, as you know.

She told Papa that it were a great pity if you did not marry for love."

"Who said I *loved* Miss Needwood?" cried Markham, conjuring up a picture of her as he had seen her on the previous evening, holding on to Lord Veren's arm. "Love that . . . that . . . malevolent ingrate! I wouldn't marry her if she were the last woman on earth!"

"How agreeable that we are of one mind in that," said a hard voice from the doorway.

Looking up, Markham found himself looking into the vivid dark of Eleanor's unforgettable eyes.

After such a confrontation, even Cecily could not feel optimistic as to a successful dénouement. And it was very strange: Now that Markham had offered her unlimited largesse and she didn't actually *need* to see Eleanor married to Markham, she found that she wished it more than ever, so fond had she become of the girl. And surely she and Markham were made for each other. Something had happened to create this misunderstanding, and she racked her brain to think what it must be. She had a sudden inspiration, her thoughts lighting for a moment on Mr. Fairfax and how Markham had voiced his disapproval over Eleanor's portrait. For sure, that was at the root of the estrangement, and if she could only persuade Eleanor to give it up, the wretch might yet be her sister.

Eleanor would not hear of canceling the sittings. Indeed, when Cecy reiterated how upset he would be, she became yet more determined to continue. So, *he* did not want to marry *her*! Well, who asked him to? Not she. Indeed, it would be her future mission in life to show him just how *much* she did not wish to marry him! She got ready for the first sitting, which had been arranged for that day, with little more than a qualm. In vain did Cecy remind her of the unsuitable nature of some of Mr. Fairfax's portraits (and goodness knows who knew about them!). In vain did she warn that now that she came to think about it, some would certainly consider it fast for an unmarried girl to sit for a single gentleman, whatever the portrait. If it would annoy Lord Markham, it must be done, for then he would be under no illusion that she was pining for his company, while he patently desired that of other females! And not only to Mr. Fairfax would she give her time. Indeed, Lord Markham would find that he would be the only man in London who could not get near her.

The sittings with Mr. Fairfax were conducted with the utmost propriety and took a week. Mr. Fairfax would have liked to have felt optimistic about Eleanor by the time the sittings were at an end, but it seemed to him that far from treating him with the distinguishing attention he had hoped for, he rarely saw her when he wasn't actually painting her. Often he had tried to keep her longer in his company by suggesting afternoon excursions, but she was always engaged elsewhere, for Lord Veren and Mr. Hervey had pretty well divided her time between them.

Far from being ostracized by society through her estrangement from Lord Markham, the ton had nothing but admiration for a girl who, having so patently fallen out with one suitor of such high degree, was able so easily to replace him with no less than three gentlemen of comparable fortune, one of whom was a marquess! "No wonder she has not contented herself with a mere viscount when she has the immediate prospect of becoming a marchioness!" whispered some among the ton.

Bu there were others, with more spiteful tongues, who prophesied a quite different fate for Eleanor and predicted that far from achieving a creditable match, all the gentlemen concerned were merely amusing themselves with her and that she would undoubtedly find herself returning to Derbyshire without having received even one offer of any worth.

In that, had they but known it, they were already mistaken. Miss Needwood had received a most unexceptionable offer, and one that, if she ever learned the details, would send Stepmama into paroxysms of frustration. The Most Honorable the Marquess of Veren had taken an opportunity, while partnering her to a water party in Islington, to present his suit. Seating Eleanor carefully in the carpeted boat and quelling all other boarders, he punted the craft out to the center of the lake, away from the sound of the orchestra, and offered his proposal in excellent form.

A few weeks before, such a proposal would have seemed the answer to all Eleanor's prayers. That she could catch the fancy of someone young, good-humored, and handsome enough to satisfy the most fastidious of young ladies, and that he should, moreover, have not only a gracious title, but should also be endowed with a handsome fortune, would have seemed a dream. But that was before she had come to know so well another young man, who had somehow managed to vanquish all other contenders, even if he *was* unaware of it! Knowing that Stepmama, and indeed most others, would consider it a piece of lunacy, Eleanor had declined Lord Veren's very flattering offer.

Not that that made any difference to his pursuit of Eleanor, since her refusal was undertaken so gently, so kindly, that he could not believe he had no chance. They parted on excellent terms, with Lord Veren's spirits undaunted. Girls always refused at first, his sisters told him. With only a little perseverance, he would certainly win his prize.

CHAPTER
15

The Honorable Miss Letitia Hervey glanced anxiously from one to another of the fashionable people gracing her mother's salon, her bosom seething with an unmaidenly sense of indignation. Mama, a sensible woman, had warned her not to expect too much, and to regard today's breakfast only as a dress rehearsal for the grand ball to be held in her honor two weeks later. The ton was notoriously unpredictable: It might find it amusing to launch Mrs. Hervey's little girl triumphantly at a mere breakfast: It might, on the other hand, decide to lie an extra hour in bed.

Mrs. Hervey needn't have worried: The house had been packed since eleven o'clock, with so many well-wishers coming and going that the breakfast was certain to rank among the season's squeezes.

That being so, it was not, then, a dearth of guests that caused Letty's chest to tighten. Nor was it the class of person that had chosen to honor her, for she had had the felicity of being kissed on the cheek by no less than three of Almack's patronesses and a royal duke—and which of them would have been considered the most important in that capricious world would have been difficult to decide. No, Letty's discontent was caused by the absence of only one person—and he was the only one in the world she cared to see. That morning, while she was being dressed in her first really grown-up gown of white *papillon* silk, with its tightly fitting corsage and delicate lace flounces, her only desire had been to see shocked amazement on Markham's face when he saw her in it. It had been a crush of some long standing, and since coming to town, she had dwelt in an enchanted dream where, on catching sight of her, he realized, in a wild, blinding moment, that nobody but Letitia Hervey must stand beside him at the altar. She had deliberately stayed out of his way since coming to town that the shock might be the more complete. And he hadn't even bothered to come!

His sister had arrived but a moment earlier, and her hopes had risen. Only to be crushed to see the Lady Cecily unfashionably attended by her husband. Even the sight of Eleanor in Lady Cecily's train did not make her pause as it might well have a week ago. *Thank goodness that rumor at least was ill founded,* she thought, remembering how all society had buzzed with the story of Markham and Eleanor on her arrival. *It would have been too hateful to have to dislike someone so nice.*

But no one, seeing Eleanor's untroubled smile as she made her way through the throng, and the pleasure with which she greeted Francis, would have given credence to the notion that she even noticed the absence of her old flame.

For Markham had vanished the capital as unpredictably as he had come. Not since the morning in Grosvenor Square had he been seen in any of his usual haunts around town: No one had clapped eyes on him at Jackson's; he had pipped no wafers at Manton's;

crossed no swords at Mr. O'Shaunessy's establishment. Friends looked for him in vain at White's and Boodles; he had placed no bets at the Royal Cockpit in Tatton Street. And the blame was all laid at Eleanor's door. For sure, she had actually rejected him, they whispered, and it was this that had sent him scurrying away from town to lick his wounds!

Eleanor knew better than anyone that the rumors circulating were entirely false, and did her best to quash them, but whenever she assured interested persons that this was so, they only put it down to the good nature and natural charity of an unaffected girl who could afford to be generous when she was courted by three eligible men! Never had her credit been higher. She was invited to every fashionable squeeze in town, and far from it being *she* who had to return home with her crest lowered, as Markham had once predicted, it seemed that *he* had been obliged to quit town.

At first, while she still smarted under the effects of their estrangement, she was glad he had gone. But now it had been more than a week since she had seen him, and in spite of the fact that Francis had taken her on a picnic to Kew, to the Royal Circus at St. George's Field, and to see the King's Guards at Hyde Park, and Lord Veren had taken up much of her time in teaching her to tool a carriage—and that without the hours spent having her portrait taken—never had a week dragged so. She looked about her, quite as eager as Letty to see him.

Cecily, too, was busy looking all around her for her brother, for she fully expected him back. All of town might not know where he had been for more than a week, but he had at least had the decency to scribble a line to furnish his sister with his destination.

Having been so royally trounced by Eleanor, and fully intending to consign all females to the devil, he had met up at Limmer's Hotel with some fellow sporting men just going off to enjoy themselves at the spring meeting at Newmarket and was persuaded to go along. He had some fuddled idea of proving to Miss Needwood that he wasn't one to hang on her sleeve. It was that, as much as anything, that on arrival at a Newmarket hostelry made him pen a message to his sister to tell her where he might be found. He was halfway through his note, when the outer door to his room suddenly swung open and two of his party pushed each other into the room.

"Come on, Markham," cried the Honorable Desmond Pakenham, a young man more renowned for the sharpness of his temper than his wit. "What the devil keeps you? We've just seen as neat a string of fillies passing by. Prettiest girls you ever saw. Tolly and myself are going to see what's to do about here. We've ordered dinner for nine, which gives us plenty of time to broach a bottle or two while we are waiting. Make a night of it. See if we can't lay on a few bets as well."

Lord Markham looked up from his note and saw at once that both must already have broached enough bottles to have given them a good start of him. The mood of enforced gaiety that had all day been buoying him up left him as suddenly as it had risen. He could foresee all too well the evening that awaited him—the sort of evening that he had put himself through countless times and lately had seemed increasingly pointless. A picture of Miss Needwood came unbidden into his head, along with the contempt she would feel at such activity.

"Go on without me," he said abruptly. "I'll catch up when this is done."

"Leave it!" said young Mr. Tollenham. "Do it later. We're all ready to go."

But Lord Markham was not to be persuaded. Adhering to his decision, the others left him to his letter, to which, however, he did not immediately return.

He sat in the fading light, leaning back in his chair with his hands crossed behind his head, the two front chair legs raised from the floor. The mood that had settled on him unaccountably depressed him.

"Drat Eleanor," he said aloud. Why couldn't he get her off his mind? She took up too many of his waking hours these days—an entirely pointless exercise since she so obviously despised him. The last words she had spoken to him still rang in his ears. In an irritation of nerves brought on entirely by hearing him say to her sister that she was the last woman on earth he would marry, Eleanor had called him an overpompous, self-satisfied idler who knew nothing of life beyond his own vanity and his own comfort. In her fury she had thrown everything at him she could think of, however unfair, finally concluding, before she stormed from the room, that he would never amount to anything while he got other people to take his responsibilities, that he would be a ne'er-do-well forever if he did not put his house in order himself instead of leaving it to others, while he played like a child. And what had been his response to her reading of his character? Why, he had immediately set off to prove how succinct it was, how faultless in every way! What was he doing here with these fellows? Fellows he hardly knew, let alone liked?

The two legs of his chair tapped noisily as they hit the deal floorboards. He ripped up the lines of handwriting before him and began on another sheet, which he had sent to his sister in Grosvenor Square. This time the message had been very different. It had told his sister that he would be out of town for a week at Arno; that he had gone to "put his house in order" and that she could reach him there if she so desired.

Thus it was that, when Cecy received the note and realized that he must have forgotten Letitia Hervey's breakfast party, she did not scruple to send him one of her sisterly missives berating him in fine style for his casual behavior to his old friends, for which his mama would never forgive him. She was pleased he was finally doing something with Arno, but still, it was all very much of a piece, she had written with her usual scant regard for the proprieties and rather unfairly, since he expected to please her. *Still* he thought only of himself, she wrote, as he proved by forgetting poor little Letty. He foisted on his family odiously vulgar women of doubtful morals (while he was incapable of appreciating perfectly *darling* girls), for he had *no taste*. He had blighted any number of young girls' come-outs, failing to notice their existence, or treating them like a Dutch uncle, which was probably even worse! And if he did so to Letty, whom he had known forever, it would be the outside of enough! She had fully expected him to take note of her words and was cross that he wasn't there.

Another lady was not altogether pleased by Markham's absence from town. Violet Pelham had broken her own rule by appearing before noon for no other reason than to track down her old lover. She was certain that even *he* could not so offend his old friends, and when she had received a careless invitation from Mr. Francis Hervey, she could not resist attending herself.

When Markham had kissed her hand at the opera house more than a week ago, he had reawoken all sorts of emotions, not the least, satisfied vanity. To have Markham making love to her in full view of the fashionable world while Eleanor looked on was quite delicious. Later, when he had escorted her home, she had expected him to stay with her, and would have welcomed him generously. She was disappointed when he didn't, though not unduly so, but when next day she heard that he had quit town and the reason society gave for it, she had been furious. To think how it must look if Markham had indeed proposed to Eleanor on the very morning after he had been seen so compromisingly with *her*! A period of reflection convinced her that society was mistaken. Whatever he was, Markham wasn't unkind. But she had come today to put that conviction to the test.

She stared over at Eleanor, irritated as much by the girl's healthy good looks as by seeing her carelessly sharing her attentions between Lord Veren, Mr. Hervey, and Orlando Fairfax, who had swarmed toward her like wasps at a picnic. And when she saw young Mr. Fairfax walk disconsolately away from Miss Needwood within a very few minutes, his shoulder hunched to show that he had had his nose put out of joint, she could not resist beckoning him over by patting the seat at her side.

"Orlando, my dear," she said, pouting and looking up at him, "why, I'd quite given up hoping you'd notice

me. How cruel of you to ignore me thus. Miss Needwood will have me scratching her eyes out for monop-
olizing all the handsome men in the room. It is too bad
of you."

"H-handsome?" said Mr. Fairfax, feeling the floppy
bow at his neck and turning a bright shade of crimson.
"L-lord, no!" he said, grinning crookedly.

"Oh, now, Orlando, don't tell me that you don't
know you are handsome . . ." She flirted with him just
as another woman might breathe, it was so much a re-
flex action, but for Orlando Fairfax, it was as a banquet
to a starving man. He'd just been made to look like a
fool in front of Eleanor by a careless, rather belittling
remark by Francis Hervey, and to hear Lady Pelham's
compliments was like a caress.

"Miss Needwood doesn't agree with you, it seems,"
he said, hunching his shoulder again.

"Oh, surely that must be wrong. She is letting you
paint her, isn't she?"

"You let me paint you," he pointed out.

"Well, there you are, then," said Lady Violet with an
expressive lift of her eyebrows.

It was true. She *had* sat for him, but only because
Countess de Lieven had done so. She hadn't known
then that the countess had done so only in compliments
to his mama, an old friend. Nor had she realized how
excruciating was his work! Her words and her tone
seemed to suggest that she had quite a different reason.

"Oh, I say," said Mr. Fairfax, fingering the bow
again.

"Miss Needwood is fortunate indeed that you have
agreed to paint her."

"Yet you didn't *take* your portrait," he reminded her.

Because I have no wish to hang a portrait that looks to have been painted by a demented child, she would have liked to reply. Instead, she said soothingly, "Ah, but I know that when you see it, you *must* think of me sometimes."

"You mean you . . . oh, I say." And this time the crimson spread right down to his neck.

"And Miss Needwood's portrait. Does it go well?"

"It is finished. Yesterday! And if I say it myself," he went on, swaggering a little, "it is one of my best. I hope I don't flatter myself, but I think few could have caught so much of Miss Needwood's special beauty. Her air of . . ."

Mr. Fairfax went on for some considerable while in this vein before he realized that he no longer had Lady Violet's attention. Looking across to where her eyes had moved, he saw that Lord Markham, looking every inch the pink of fashion, had that moment come through the doors into the salon.

As Letty saw him walk into her mama's salon, she felt that she would never know a sweeter moment. It was to become even sweeter, for he walked straight past Miss Needwood without a flicker of recognition, not pausing until he reached Letty. Much as she liked Eleanor, she would have been less than human had she not savored the moment.

Throwing just a brief look at Lady Cecily as if to underline how mistaken she was as to his character, he said for the benefit of the whole room, "Letty, how lovely you look. I've dashed back to town so as not to miss your come-out, and I can say only that it was worth every mile."

"Oh, Markham," Letty said, smiling mistily and staring up at him as he took her hand. "I thought you'd forgotten."

"Forgotten? What kind of a loose screw do you take me for?" he said, showing no disposition to let go of her hand. "Wild horses couldn't have kept me away."

"It was the tame ones I was afraid of," Letty drolly explained. "Everyone said you were at Newmarket."

"Newmarket? No, I've been at Arno supervising some drainage I've put in hand," he said, determined to make his sister eat her words, "but I'm surprised you had time to notice. A pretty girl like you must be besieged with admirers. I reckon I've come back not a moment too soon."

She blushed at the compliment, not trusting herself to answer, while Cecily looked on indignantly. It was true that she had rung a peal over her brother about his careless behavior to debutantes and that she had reminded him about Letty, but there was no need to lay it on with a trowel! He would be raising hopes he had no intention of satisfying if he were not careful. And to have him ignoring Eleanor was more than she could stand.

"You have not said hello to Miss Needwood, brother," she said sweetly, seeing Markham continue to hang over Letitia Hervey as one demented!

"Ah, Miss Needwood. There you are. Forgive me. I didn't see you. I hope you continue to enjoy town?" he said politely.

"Perfectly, sir," Eleanor replied, equally distant.

"Excellent," said Markham. Then, turning back to Letty, he said warmly, "I had better get in before the others, Letty. Will you do me the very great honor of allowing me to drive you to St. James's Park tomorrow, if the weather holds?"

Eleanor, her face suffused with color, would have liked to slap him! St. James's was *their* place. She turned away at once to continue a conversation with the marquess that Markham's entry had interrupted, her head almost bursting with the effort to appear nonchalant.

Lady Violet, meanwhile watching from the other side of the room, caught entirely the wrong end of the stick! She saw only that instead of coming across to her side, Markham had joined Eleanor, and that after all the fuss at the opera that had set tongues wagging. So he had been using her, after all. A rather unpleasant little smile lit her face. It was too bad of him. She knew a sudden spurt of annoyance against him, even a little anger, though she rarely allowed her emotions to make her uncomfortable. Yet Markham really had been rather naughty! Certainly she would have to look for a chance to make him feel just a bit of a fool, as he had made her!

Mr. Fairfax, meanwhile, was still going on about his portrait of Eleanor, and to Violet's distinct amusement, his words suggested an opportunity for her revenge almost at once. It really was rather a *wicked* scheme, just a little naughty. And Markham would hate it. She interrupted Mr. Fairfax in full flight.

"You know, Orlando, one can't help but admire Miss Needwood. Such perfection of face. Such perfection of form."

"Eh?" he said in surprise. "Shouldn't have thought

you'd like her much. Weren't you and Markham . . . ?"
He petered off at her raised eyebrow.

"Lord, that was eons ago, my child," she said with
studied indifference. "I have nothing against Miss
Needwood. Indeed, it delights one just to look at such
a beautiful creature, doesn't it? She almost reminds one
of the nymphs one sees in ancient paintings. What happiness it must have been for you to paint her. And how
frustrating for such an artist as yourself."

"Er, oh? Frustrating?"

"But yes! That beautiful form. And to have it hidden
by mere convention. How you must have wished to be
able to . . . pull aside the curtain."

Mr. Fairfax blushed a fiery red. "I assure you,
ma'am, that I did not for one instant—"

"Of course you didn't. Your sensitivity is such that I
do not suppose for one moment that you would allow
yourself to— Yet"—and here she allowed herself a little
shrug—"and yet an artist is not as other men. Especially
one as gifted as yourself." Another shrug, very expressive. "Indeed, Orlando, one might almost say that in not
'pulling aside the curtain' such a man sins against his
talents. Can one imagine Michelangelo failing to cap-
ture Eve? Or Botticelli refusing to paint Venus?"

"But Miss Needwood would never—"

She held up her hand and shook her head slowly. "Of
course she wouldn't, dear boy. But why need she know?
You have the other portrait for the likeness, and surely
your imagination is such that . . ."

"But what would people think?"

"People! I don't suggest that you hang it in the Royal
Academy," she said soothingly. "It would be a portrait
for your private collection, of course. But there! Think

161

no more about it. I can see that you don't like the idea. I can only honor such delicacy, however misplaced. But, oh, what an omission for posterity."

She had the satisfaction of leaving him with a very thoughtful expression on his face, certain that her wicked scheme had fallen on fertile ground.

CHAPTER

16

"What can you be about, Markham?" his sister reproached him. "To raise hopes you have no intention of satisfying. And in Letty, of all people. Little more than a child. It was not well done of you. Not well done at all!"

Lady Cecily was in high dudgeon. Having asked Letty to go and drive out with him on the morrow, he had taken leave of her party within half an hour and it had afterward taken Lady Cecily most of the afternoon to track him down. It was not in the lady's scheme of things to be inconvenienced in such a way, and having bullied him into returning with them to St. James's Square, she was now laying into him with the broad side of her tongue.

Lord Markham disarmed her at once by saying humbly, "You are quite right. It was *not* very well done of me at all. I don't know what I was about."

"Why did you, then, Markham? And what have you been up to, going to Arno at such a time?"

"I went up to do what I should have done years ago. Send Bates packing."

"No! How did you dare? What will Papa say?" asked

Cecily, awed. "You have not turned him off without a new post to go to?"

"As a matter of fact, I was able to put him in the way of an excellent position with old Faveringham. I knew he'd been wanting a reliable man for several months now, and Bates will do the job very well without m'father breathing down his neck."

"Oh, Markham! Wait till I tell Hart! I still don't know how you dared."

"T'was you told me to do it!" replied Lord Markham indignantly, though he knew very well that he had done it not at the instigation of his sister, but because of the apparent contempt of quite another female.

"You won't tell Papa that, will you?" cried Cecily, going pale.

"Of course not," Markham replied. "I shall take all the blame to myself, I assure you. As a matter of fact, I can't wait to do so!"

"Doesn't Papa know yet?" Cecy asked nervously.

"Not yet," he said evenly. "I shall ride to Fildes later this week and tell him face-to-face. I owe him that much, at least. And I shall tell him, too, that I've started draining the lower pasture."

"No! Have you indeed? But Papa said—"

"Arno does not belong to Papa, it belongs to me," he said firmly. "I shall decide what is best for it."

"You will need a steward, dearest," his sister said tentatively in face of this new and rather splendid brother.

"Oh, certainly," Markham replied with a grim smile. "But he'll be of *my* choosing, and I'll not be in a hurry to make a mistake."

His sister threw her arms around his neck and gave

him a sisterly hug. "I'm proud of you, my love," she said, adding with a little alarm, "but you promise you won't say it was my idea, don't you?"

"I've already said so, love. I mean to stand on my own two feet at last. I came back only to catch Letty's come-out, as you bid me."

It was unlucky to mention Letty, for it brought Cecily back to a sense of her grievance. Much as she was proud of him about Arno, she could not help reminding him, "You have never said what has made you ask Letty to go driving with you."

"What did you expect after your letter? You told me I had to notice her! I thought you'd be pleased," he protested.

"You thought nothing of the sort! You have no pretension there, have you?" She looked up at him sharply.

For a moment he was tempted to pretend he had. If one of his reasons for ferrying Letty about was to make his sister eat her words, another, and by far the greater, was to show Miss Needwood that he could get heiresses quite as easily as she could bring rich young men to heel! A moment's reflection showed him what a coxcomb he would be if he followed that pattern with a child like Letty, and he said peevishly, "Don't be absurd."

"Then you must stop it straightaway," said Cecily quietly. "Only goodness knows how it's to be done, for it'll hurt her feelings if you cancel."

"Cancel! Of course I shan't cancel. Leave it to me," he said with a sigh. "I shall leave Letty's heart and her pride intact. I shall think of a way to do it."

Vauxhall Gardens, that "delightful and much frequented place of summer amusement," was situated

165

about a mile and a half from London on the south side of Lambeth. Formerly little more than a tea garden enlivened by orchestra music, its rural beauty and extra attractions now made it so popular that it is not surprising that on its opening gala night, which occurred nearly a week after Letty's come-out, Cecily and Hartley made up a party of friends to take Eleanor there to see the new walks and transparent paintings.

A party of ten had been made up, a party that included among other friends the Marquess of Veren, who much hoped to get Eleanor to himself and try another proposal.

Mr. Fairfax had included himself. Now that Eleanor's painting was completed—she had promised to hang it in her papa's house when she returned home—he found it difficult to get to see her. She found his company so tiresome that she always found an excuse when he invited her out, and unless he could hang on to the crowd about her was unable to get near her. Indeed, he had even begun to wonder if he was wasting his time.

Eleanor herself had insisted that Veren be invited, for she intended to show Lord Markham, whom she knew had been asked, that if he preferred Letitia Hervey's company to her own, she could well be amused without him. But Markham had sent his apologies, and even while she looked on the entrancing scene all around her, she felt so lethargic that had she not been determined to hide it, those who knew her best and were used to her high spirits would have been surprised indeed.

Having taken an apartment in the painted pavilion built for the late Prince of Wales from which they could watch the orchestra, they had the felicity of meeting up with Francis Hervey "doing the pretty," as he said, and escorting his mama and his sister to the same entertainment. It was very natural for the parties to merge, much as Lord Veren might regret it, and Eleanor was soon seated between the two of them, being diverted by their nonsense.

Lord Veren might protest at Mr. Hervey's presence, but he really had little to worry about in his company. Francis had had a delightful flirtation with Miss Needwood, just as he had promised Markham, but he had no intention at all of taking things further. He thought her a charming girl, but his greatest enjoyment in her company was putting out of joint the noses of other admirers. Lord Veren, on the other hand, was increasingly smitten, so far so that he had even brought his mama to town to meet Eleanor. The dowager, known for being a high stickler, had been fully expected to rout Miss Needwood as she had routed all former aspirants. But Lady Jersey had just whispered in her ear that the Earl and Countess of Fildes considered her good enough for Markham, which gave her pause for thought, and she found herself pleasantly surprised by the girl's unaffected manner. She gave her son to understand that she had no objection to the match regardless of the disparity in fortune, and since Veren had already decided that he would not let it stop him if she had, he continued to pursue Eleanor with a determination that had people expecting the match to be announced anytime.

Veren was presently engaged in getting Eleanor away from Mr. Hervey. Mr. Fairfax, meanwhile, could not get near her and found himself instead seated by Miss Letitia Hervey. He was too well brought up to show

how much he regretted his partner, and soon had Letty quite at her ease.

Inevitably he asked the question, "And how are you enjoying your first season, Miss Hervey?"

"Oh, it is of all things delightful," replied Letty. "Why, I have been . . . everywhere." Her voice dwindled strangely.

He could not help noticing the sad note, and was puzzled. Wasn't it said that she was Markham's latest flirt? Shouldn't that be enough to have her in the heights? He determined to try to find out what was wrong.

"You must be the envy of half London, Miss Hervey," he said, feeling his way. "You have been much admired, I'm told, and—I haven't got this wrong, have I?—you have become rather . . . thick with Markham. People talk of you being seen everywhere together. That is a triumph indeed for a young girl like yourself."

"Oh, yes, indeed!" said Letty brightly. "Mama says I am the most fortunate girl in town. And . . . and who would not wish to be escorted by Markham? He has been everything kind. Indeed, yes!" Her effusions stopped suddenly, and she looked rather pensive for a moment, beginning at last with, "Only I did not precisely realize that Lord Markham was so . . . so . . . *learned*!"

"*Is he?* Markham? Are you sure?"

"Why, yes, indeed," replied Letty earnestly, "for only think, he has taken me out four times: first to St. James's Park. I had thought we were going to see the gardens," she confided, "but he took me instead to see the private collection at the queen's palace. He said I must not miss seeing Mr. Benjamin West's painting of the death of General Wolfe, which is thought very fine.

168

He . . . he . . . carries a little guidebook everywhere, so we won't overlook anything important!"

"Good God," said Fairfax in disgust. "What a flat!"

"I can see you are surprised, as I was myself. But it is very kind of him, is it not? Secondly we visited the Leverian Museum, more especially the Sandwich room, dedicated to the memory of Captain Cook. He seemed to find it quite . . . quite . . . elevating! Our third outing found us at the Royal Academy, for he says that no young lady can afford to be behindhand in her knowledge of the arts . . . though I regret to say that I . . . And four hours was quite . . ." She petered off sadly, then collected her thread of thought. "And finally he was so good as to take me to"—a manful swallow ensued, and she went on—"to Bullock's Museum to see Napoleon's traveling chaise. He says I must not miss the chance to see an artifact belonging to the . . . monster that cut down the . . . the finest flower of English manhood."

"Good Lord!" said Mr. Fairfax indignantly, wishing Lord Markham, not for the first time, to hell.

"It is *particularly* kind of him to spend so much time with me . . . and . . . naturally . . . one had much rather be improving one's mind than . . . than going to such frivolous places as . . . as . . . Astley's Amphitheater, or . . . or to see the Invisible Girl at Leicester Square . . . or the Automatical Exhibition in St. Martin's Lane . . . even if one does have to miss seeing the mechanical figure that dances on a tightrope."

At the sign of so much misery, Mr. Fairfax could not prevent himself from giving Letty's hand a gentle squeeze. He was sure a tear trembled on her eyelash.

His attention strayed for a moment over to where Eleanor, apparently perfectly well entertained, continued to talk to the marquess without a thought for him. "Miss Hervey," he said suddenly. "Would you like to go to St. Martin's Lane to see the Automatical Exhibition?"

She looked up at him, her eyes still sparkling with tears. "Oh! I should love it of all things, Mr. Fairfax," she cried unhesitatingly, and it was agreed between them that if her mama consented, he would take her the following day.

The interval just then beginning, the two parties were obliged to separate since the Herveys had bespoken supper in their box and the others had arranged for it in the piazza.

Mrs. Hervey came across to place a shawl around her daughter's shoulders, and before they parted, permission was sought by Mr. Fairfax and graciously given— Mrs. Hervey being quite intelligent enough not to reject advances from any eligible partner. She expressed herself delighted for Letty to have such a treat and knew that she could trust her little girl to him without a qualm!

As they passed through the rotunda on their way to the piazza, Mr. Fairfax heard his name called and had the felicity of meeting with another old friend. Lady Violet Pelham was there with Lord James FitzSimmons, a new conquest. Waving Lord James cavalierly in the direction of the refreshments and bidding him find them a seat, she took Orlando to one side.

"My dear, tell me. I couldn't help asking," she said quietly, making sure they were out of earshot of all. "Did you tackle that painting we spoke of at all?"

Orlando blushed to his ear tips.

"I . . . I did attempt something of the sort," he said

noncommittedly, feeling suddenly rather uncomfortable. "Finished it yesterday, as a matter of fact, though I'm not so sure it was such a . . ."

"Oh, my dear. Don't disappoint me. Such an artist as you are. Such a talent," she said throatily. "You are not to be confined by such common prejudices. And how I should love to see it."

But Orlando, having so recently left her, had suddenly a picture of Miss Hervey in front of him, though it was Eleanor he had painted. What would a little innocent like Miss Hervey think of him painting such a portrait of Eleanor? She would be disgusted! She *should* be disgusted! He found himself going hot at the thought that she might find out, and the absolute conviction that he had done something quite unforgivable struck him forcibly for the first time. How had he come to let himself be persuaded?

"Indeed, Lady Violet," he said in sudden panic, "I pray you not to mention that painting to anyone. It . . . it was a mistake . . . I shouldn't have . . ."

"Orlando, how serious you are! Is the picture, then, so shocking?"

"No, indeed, ma'am. I deliberately . . . toned down what we spoke of," he said delicately.

"Toned it down? How intriguing."

"I was not certain I had the right to . . . to what you felt my art entitled me," he explained, tying himself in knots. "My own . . . delicacy . . . forbade me taking such—in short, I did not feel it permissible to have Miss Needwood's form so entirely exposed. In view of her not being in—"

"What *did* you do, Orlando," asked Lady Violet impatiently.

"I painted her as we said, but I used a quantity of draperies to good effect. Diaphanous draperies, but quite sufficient so that there is but a hint ... a very slight hint, of color through them. It would be a high stickler indeed who would find anything to blame in such a portrait."

"Indeed, yes," agreed the lady, "though there *are* such sticklers, Orlando."

He noticed that there was a very odd look on Lady Violet's face, almost a smile. He couldn't quite say why, but he had the strangest feeling he was being manipulated. He said very firmly, with a confidence he was far from feeling, "However innocent we know the portrait to be, I suspect you are right. But I can trust you not to let so much as a whisper of it pass your lips, Lady Violet. Indeed, I begin to think it was a bad project. Perhaps it would be better if I destroyed the painting altogether. More seemly. I should not like to— Yes, that would be quite the best. I shall destroy it." And he went off after his party without another word, looking very thoughtful.

Lady Violet, too, was thoughtful. Destroy the painting? That would not at all suit her.

Two mornings after the gala night at Vauxhall Gardens, Mrs. Fairfax, at her Friday at-home, received an unexpected visitor. Lady Violet Pelham called on Mrs. Fairfax very early, indeed, much earlier than was usual at an at-home. She was received by Dassett at the front door, and having with her her man of affairs, Dassett could not help showing his surprise.

"It's all right, Dassett," said Lady Violet, waving him to one side. "Edwards is here with me to collect my portrait. You must have been told to expect me. I have been meaning to during these past weeks and simply haven't found the time. Oh, no," she continued, seeing Dassett turn toward the studio, "do not you bother with it. Edwards can do it. He knows where the studio is. I know how busy you must be today preparing for Mrs. Fairfax's visitors. Tiresome of me to want it now. Edwards has brought a cloth to cover it. Ah, my dear Mrs. Fairfax"—Mrs. Fairfax, overhearing voices in the hallway, had come to investigate—"I have but this moment told Dassett not to put himself out. I thought to collect my portrait now that I have prepared a place for it, for I know how dearest Orlando wishes it! But Edwards can see to it, you know, quite easily."

"Lady Violet! How charming. And your portrait, too. Of course! And if Edwards *could* possibly see to it, it would be a help. I need Dassett just now. I want him to place a table for me. . . ."

"Of course, my dear," said Lady Violet, taking Mrs. Fairfax's hand between both of hers. Then with a meaningful look at Edwards, she went with her and Dassett into the salon.

CHAPTER

17

When Mr. Orlando Fairfax returned home early that evening, he was feeling decidedly happy. He had that day been on his second expedition with Miss Hervey, this time to the gardens at Kew, and had found her a bewitching companion. Remembering the look of delight with which she had received a little sketch he had executed of her in the midst of the flowers there, an attractive smile played about his mouth. Miss Hervey was so—so different from the other girls he had known. So often they made him feel like a mere boy: Miss Hervey, on the other hand, seemed to rely on him for common sense, and looked up at him with adoring eyes. Never had he spent two days more pleasantly, and he looked forward optimistically to more such days—indeed, an endless stream of such days. He went in to seek Mama, for he did not wish her to be kept in ignorance of his new love for a moment longer than necessary.

He found her in the salon, and in his happiness dropped a kiss on her forehead.

"Ah, there you are, my dear," said his mama, looking up from her embroidery. "Have you had a good day? Dassett and I have been rushed off our feet. So many callers, you would not believe."

"You have not tired yourself, Mama?" replied Fairfax anxiously, for in spite of the impression he had managed to give Eleanor, he was a fond enough son when it caused him no effort, and he *was* in a particularly good humor.

"Indeed, no, dear," she replied with truth, "for Dassett has seen to everything quite as usual. And how did Miss Needwood enjoy her day?"

"I did not take Miss Needwood, Mama," replied Fairfax with a slight lessening of patience. "You remember. I took Miss Hervey."

"Did you, my dear? Well, to be sure, I had thought . . . do I know her, Orlando?"

"Not yet, Mama, but I intend that you should, for she is the sweetest girl imaginable. You will like her of all things."

"I'm sure I shall, dearest," Mrs. Fairfax replied, patting his hand comfortably, "for you said the same about Miss Needwood, and she was charming."

Mr. Fairfax had the grace to look discomfited. "I believe I did say something of the sort about Miss Needwood, Mama," he said gravely, "but that was in a very general way. Very general, you understand. I admired Miss Needwood's beauty, but there was really nothing in it."

"Nothing? Well, to be sure, how very strange. I was certain you . . . but there! You know what a muddle my mind is. And so, Miss Hervey is lovely?"

"She really is, Mama. We have spent such a pleasant day. I intend to see a lot more of her."

"How nice, Orlando—and oh! that reminds me, I have something else to cheer you up, darling. Lady Pelham came to my at-home this morning and has collected her portrait at last. She has been waiting only until she had prepared a proper place for it—and you thought she did not care for it."

"Collected it, has she?" He looked pleased.

"Yes, dear—and so thoughtful. Knowing it to be my at-home, she brought a man with her so that Dassett wouldn't have to see to it. We had a delightful coze while Edwards collected it from your studio. I like Lady Violet. She speaks nice and slowly."

He was only half listening, for his mother's words made him recollect his last meeting with Lady Violet and reminded him of what he had now come to regard as the infamous portrait of Miss Needwood. In all the enjoyment of taking Miss Hervey out, he'd forgotten all about it, and about his decision to destroy it. He determined to do so at once, and cutting across his mama's conversation, he mounted the stairs to his studio to accomplish it.

Because of the nature of the painting, he had been somewhat secretive in its execution, working mostly quite late, and as soon as the paint was sufficiently dry, covering the easel with a large cloth.

Pausing only to put on his painting smock and collect some whitewash, ready to paint over the canvas, he pulled aside the cloth—to find that instead of Miss Needwood, he was confronted with a still life of a bowl of cherries! He did not immediately take in the full import of what had occurred. For sure, he must have moved Miss Needwood's portrait. Or, perhaps, Dassett had. He looked behind one or two paintings that stood against his walls to see if he had, in a lapse of concentration, put it there, but found no joy. Panic began in earnest to build up, and he was soon flicking rapidly through all his work, dashing from one place to another in apprehension. He called Dassett, but Dassett had no light to shed on the matter, except to say very diffidently that "to be sure, Lady Pelham's man had been in the studio, but he was sure he would not . . ." etc.

It would not do to be taking servants into one's confidence, and collecting his dignity, he dismissed Dassett calmly with, "Of course not. I have but misplaced it, I daresay. No great thing."

But when Dassett had gone, it was a different tale. How could he help but remember that Lady Violet had asked about that painting two days since? How could he help remembering her look of disappointment when he said he would destroy it? He dashed down again to his mama, and knelt beside her, taking her hand into his.

"Mama," he said, forcing himself to speak calmly and slowly. "You were saying something about Lady Violet. Am I to understand that her servant removed the portrait from the studio himself? Dassett helped him, I imagine? He wasn't alone?"

"No, dear, that was what was so particularly agreeable. Lady Violet knew how busy Dassett would be of a Friday and brought Edwards with her. She would not even let Dassett help, which I thought so considerate, for I needed him myself. Edwards simply went to the studio and took it away, which was just as well, for Miss Barkett and Lady Sefton arrived at that very moment, and with all the coming and going . . ."

Without waiting for her to finish her narrative, he dashed upstairs to the studio again and looked through his paintings, this time much more slowly and thoroughly, until he had satisfied himself beyond doubt that the painting had gone. And the thought that it must have been Lady Violet's man who took it was not long in following.

But why? Why should she take it? He cast his mind back again to Vauxhall Gardens. She had not liked it when he had said he would destroy it, of that there could be no doubt. And she had expressed such a desire to see it! For sure, that must be it. She had taken it from curiosity. To see what he had made of it. She saw something to admire in his work if others didn't, and she didn't wish it to be wasted. The thought was so delicious that he began to feel a deal more cheerful. The easy vanity puffed itself up. He must go and see the dear woman and get back the portrait. Even if she pleaded with him to keep it—a very pleasant image—the painting must be destroyed. He should make her understand that. But there was no denying that it was gratifying indeed to have an admirer willing to go to such lengths for a viewing of one of his works.

He was so fortunate as to find Lady Violet at home, and she was quite alone. Without preamble he demanded the painting. He quite understood the temptation; indeed, he honored her courage in being so unconventional, but really she must ... she *must* give him it back. This last was said in gentle sadness.

"Take a painting? Whatever can you mean, Mr. Fairfax?" Lady Violet blankly replied. "I haven't a notion what you are talking about."

"But your man entered my studio this morning," said Orlando in sudden horror at the abyss opening up before him. "And now the painting of Miss Needwood is gone."

"Do you think Edwards has it?" said Violet, willfully

misunderstanding, and enjoying herself hugely. "But how intriguing. I shall send for him at once, shall I?"

"Yes—no—dash it all, you *know* he took it on your instructions," he replied hotly, his manners deserting him. "You wanted to see it. You said so."

"I wanted to see it, but not as much as that," she said, laughing. "Not enough to steal it, you silly boy. What should I want with such a painting? Edwards did take a painting from your studio, but it was the one of myself, naturally. I thought I was to have it. As for this other painting, I am at a loss to explain it. Has it indeed gone? How dreadful."

Something in her attitude, some slight amusement in her eyes and around her mouth that she was unable quite to suppress, told him that she knew precisely how to explain his loss and had certainly done the deed! But how did one call a lady a liar? One didn't. Less than five minutes later, minutes during which Lady Pelham had heartily amused herself at his expense by putting up ridiculous explanations of the portrait's disappearance while he seethed inside, he found himself bowing his way out of the salon, having even apologized for disturbing her.

He stood on the corner of Jermyn and Duke streets, clutching his head in his hands and cursing himself for a fool for having been so easily manipulated by such a woman. The picture had been made at her prompting all along. She had flattered him into it. But why? What did she intend to do with it? What *could* she do with it?

He found himself thinking back to the painting and went hot with embarrassment. Such a very warm painting would ruin Miss Needwood—for who would believe she hadn't sat for it? Enough tongues had wagged even when she consented to sit for a respectable painting. For sure Lady Pelham intended harm to Miss Needwood—though he was entirely at a loss to know why. Why hadn't he destroyed it when he said he would? But he'd been so taken up with Miss Hervey these past two days, he hadn't given it a thought.

Recollection of Miss Hervey seemed to depress him further, for it became apparent, quite abruptly, what he must do. His outings with Miss Hervey—those very outings on which he had fixed so much future happiness—must cease. Indeed, Miss Hervey herself must become a source of regret (probably eternal regret!) to him. No matter how little he now might relish the idea, he must offer Eleanor Needwood his heart and home—and save both their reputations.

Less than an hour later, Mr. Fairfax was on his knees in front of Eleanor, offering his proposals in form, having persuaded Lady Cecily that the violence of his feelings could no longer be denied. However much Cecily wished for Eleanor to marry Markham, there was no denying that that promising relationship had lately gone sadly awry, and she was too much a woman of the world not to encourage Eleanor to get such a fortune as Fairfax's if she could. Despite Eleanor's earnest pleas to the contrary, she had left them alone together to allow Mr. Fairfax to pursue his suit.

"Oh, do get up, Mr. Fairfax. Do!" cried Eleanor crossly before he had time to say so much as a word in his behalf.

Eleanor had had a most trying day and was in no mood to be patient with Orlando. In the past few hours she had had the flattering distinction of refusing yet another offer from Veren and, at the other end of the scale, had had the exquisite misery of being cut by Lord Markham when their carriages had passed in Green Park. As if that were not enough, Mr. Hervey, too, continued to flirt with her, though he had said himself that he wasn't the marrying kind. Really, there was no understanding men.

And now, to have this ninnyhammer on his knees before her was giving her a headache.

"Orlando, do get up," she said again more sternly, "else I shall leave the room." Indeed, she made to take one or two steps toward the door, only to find his hands grasping unaccountably the bottom of her skirts.

"Miss Needwood, you shall, you *must* listen to me," he gasped desperately. "You must allow me—"

"Stop that at once, Mr. Fairfax," cried Eleanor crossly, and every other word was punctuated with a sharp slap on top of Orlando's head with her open hand.

"But, Eleanor," Mr. Fairfax protested, letting go of her skirts and holding his hands up to protect himself. "You don't understand."

"My name, Mr. Fairfax, is Miss Needwood," she said frostily. "And I understand only too well."

"If you would just give me time to explain," he said miserably, "you will come to see that you have no choice."

"No choice? Of course I have a choice, Mr. Fairfax. I may even choose not to marry *anybody* after my experiences in London!"

To her surprise, she thought she heard him mumble something that sounded very much like "painting."

"I beg your pardon, Mr. Fairfax. I did not quite catch . . ."

"There is the painting, you see," he explained unhappily.

"My painting? Pray what has my painting to do with anything?" she replied rather more kindly, remembering how she had used him. "You have painted me. That is all. That gives you no right to hope whatever."

"Not *that* painting. It is the . . . the other one," said Orlando, swallowing hard.

Eleanor's brows lowered. "Other one?" she said, staring hard at him. "You have me completely confused, Mr. Fairfax. What other one?"

"I . . . I painted two portraits," he explained, his words almost disappearing into his neckcloth.

"Did you? How odd. Why did you never show me the other?"

"It . . . it was not . . . precisely . . . the sort of painting you would have . . . liked to . . ." He petered off miserably.

"Describe the painting, if you please," said Eleanor, his palpable discomfort making her suddenly very suspicious.

"It . . . it is rather . . . difficult, you see . . ."

"Then I suggest you try very hard," said Eleanor sweetly.

"I may as well tell you at once that you won't like it," said Mr. Fairfax solemnly.

"And still you haven't told me *anything*," she cried.

Mr. Fairfax steeled himself, and then, letting it all out in a rush, said, "I painted a portrait of you as a . . . as a nymph."

"As a nymph? How odd! I cannot think anyone less like a nymph than myself. But why should I not see it?" Her voice was all interest.

182

"I . . . I thought you might not entirely like it, you see," said Mr. Fairfax starkly.

"So much you have said, but why should not I?"

Mr. Fairfax embarked at once on an intellectual explanation of the conventions habitually observed in the depiction of nymphs, in which, though Eleanor comprehended but one word in three, he so often mentioned "diaphanous" that she was suspicious.

"Mr. Fairfax, I feel myself dangerously angry. At once, if you please! In what garb did you paint me?"

Orlando coughed slightly and straightened his shoulders. "Dear lady, you are thinking far more than the reality, I am persuaded. The merest suggestion of . . . and made entirely proper by the use of diaphanous materials . . ."

"I shall run mad if you do not tell me!" She took several steps nearer, clenched her fists, and turned away. "What was I wearing in this painting?"

"You were a nymph, Miss Needwood," said Mr. Fairfax, as if that explained it all.

Eleanor took a deep breath. "Did you dare to paint me without . . ." She could not bear to say the words, but they were unnecessary, since Mr. Fairfax nodded his head unhappily.

"You painted me—like that?" Scarcely can a voice have sounded so shrill.

"But there was only the suggestion, Miss Needwood," said Mr. Fairfax, trying to be perfectly fair to himself. "Nobody can actually see . . . see . . . anything!"

Mr. Fairfax retreated to a safer distance and repeated his sentence, at which Eleanor swiftly covered the ground between them.

"You! You!" Her words were interspersed by her hands trying to reach him.

Edging away from her all the time, Mr. Fairfax hurried to reassure her. "Miss Needwood, you are overwrought. Really, the picture is unexceptionable! My own respect for you would never allow . . ."

"Respect!"

"Every care was taken to preserve respectability, I assure you."

"And all this was done to make me agree to marry you!" cried Eleanor in shocked tones. "I never heard anything like. What sort of man are you to think of such a thing? Surely you must see that if you wished so much to marry me, this is not the way to persuade me."

"But I don't *want* to marry you," cried Mr. Fairfax indignantly. "I am asking you only for your sake."

Eleanor's eyebrows shot up, and she gave a mighty swipe at his head, which fortunately for him missed by a mile. "How *dare* you insult me," she cried passionately.

"I'm not insulting you!" cried Mr. Fairfax. And then, dropping to one knee, albeit still behind the divan, he said valiantly, "Asking you, sweet lady, to . . . to make me the happiest of men. Assure you I'll do all in my power to . . ."

"Are you mad! You are the last person in the world I should wish to marry," she shrieked in tones of revulsion. "You are a . . . a worm . . . a . . . toad!"

"I do not greatly care what you think me," Mr. Fairfax, coming to the end of his tether, hotly replied. "It may surprise you to know that you are not first oars with me, either!"

"Then why did you paint such a . . . such a *loathsome*

painting? Goodness, Mr. Fairfax, I cannot even *imagine* anybody wishing to do such a thing."

At this very just recrimination, Mr. Fairfax seemed to deflate, just like a balloon, and he got up from his knees and seated himself despondently on a chair. "Because I'm a fool, that is why," he said miserably, crossing one leg over the other and resting his chin in his hand.

"That goes without saying," replied Eleanor, feeling only marginally appeased. "But still it doesn't explain what made you do such a thing. It is the most . . . the most ungentlemanly thing I ever heard of."

"If you will listen without hitting me, I'll tell you," Fairfax said, aggrieved.

Eleanor sat down on the divan.

"Fold your hands, too," said Fairfax, eyeing her with hostility.

Eleanor raised her eyes, but did as she was bid.

"It was at Miss Hervey's come-out," he explained miserably. "I was speaking to Lady Pelham about your portrait. I painted her, too, and she was naturally interested in hearing how it was coming along."

"She would be, of course," said Eleanor, unable to exclude the sarcasm from her voice. "Bated breath, I shouldn't wonder."

"It was Lady Pelham's idea that I should paint you au naturel," said Mr. Fairfax, eager to have it understood.

"Oh, don't be so ridiculous," said Eleanor. "Why should she?"

"Well, that's what I don't know," he exclaimed. "I've given the matter no end of thought, but I'm dashed if I can come up with a really good reason. It didn't occur to me at the time, but it's deuced odd, isn't it? You and Lady Pelham have not quarreled, have you?"

"I hardly *know* her. I've spoken to her only once or twice, and then only because she has come up to speak to Lord Markham, for I believe him to be an acquaintance of hers."

Mr. Fairfax put his head in his hands. "Oh, Lord! That's it, isn't it!"

"What do you mean, Mr. Fairfax," Eleanor asked impatiently.

"I'd forgotten all about it, but Lady Violet and Markham were thick as thieves about six months back. I even mentioned it to her that day. And they do say she never likes to give up her admirers. This would be just the sort of thing to amuse the lady, though she assured me it was all over between them. A fine thing for Markham to swallow if he was shown to have been chasing a girl who was willing to pose for *that* kind of portrait. And now that I think of it, Lady Violet was deuced disappointed when I told her I'd added draperies for decency! It would have suited her purpose far better had I followed her wishes more nearly. Markham would have been furious. Imagine what his father would say!"

"I *didn't* pose for it," said Eleanor, ominously quiet.

"But who will believe it?" asked Fairfax rationally.

Eleanor stood up and uttered a quiet scream. Then she strode up and down the room, thinking. She suddenly came to a stop. "Mr. Fairfax, I'm confused again. Why don't you just burn the painting? Without the painting it will be your word against Lady Pelham's."

Mr. Fairfax removed himself from his chair and retreated once more behind the divan. "You won't like this, either," he told her sadly, "so I'd prefer it if you remain that side of the divan."

"Oh, do go on, Orlando, for goodness' sake!"

"The painting has been stolen from my studio, and I am pretty certain that Lady Pelham has it to make mischief with," he replied, letting it tumble out.

Eleanor sank heavily down on the divan and said not a word for more than a minute. So worried was he about her that Mr. Fairfax came around and sank on his knee before her, chafing her hands.

"Now it's all right, Eleanor," he said kindly. "There's nothing to worry about. If we marry, who can say anything? A man can paint his wife any way he pleases."

"Wife! You are joking me, Mr. Fairfax! I am not your wife, nor have I any intention of so becoming."

"But the painting!"

"What do you think Lady Pelham will do with the painting?" asked Eleanor nervously.

"I don't know," Mr. Fairfax pensively replied. Then, brightening, he said, "Perhaps she will only show it to Lord Markham. I don't see how she can show it elsewhere, for she denied having it."

"Show it to Markham! I'd die sooner!" said Eleanor tightly. "Mr. Fairfax, we must retrieve that painting—and it must be done tonight, before she has a chance to show it to . . . to . . . anyone!"

"Aye, so we must," he agreed at once. "Get it back. Just so."

"If Lady Pelham wishes to play at games, then she has come to the right person. I am not one of your milk-and-water misses, as she will soon find out. If she can

187

steal it from you, we can steal it back again. After all, it is *your* painting. She has no right to it."

"Aye, so it is," he said, brightening. "But how *can* we get it? She had an excuse for getting into my studio. We have no excuse for getting into her house. And besides, we don't know where she has put it, do we? I can hardly go up to the door and say I want to have a look around, can I?"

"How big is the painting?" Eleanor asked.

"The same size as the other, why?"

"There can't be so many places to put such a large object, can there? She'll have put it somewhere where no casual observer can see it. Her boudoir or her bedroom. We must get into her boudoir somehow."

"Get to her boudoir, oh, is that all? And just how do you propose to do that?"

"Why, through the window, naturally. After all the servants have gone to bed."

"After all the—you must be mad!"

"Mr. Fairfax, if I don't get that painting back, I shall be ruined. If you won't help me, I shall have to do it alone."

"I didn't say I wouldn't help you," said Orlando, hunching his shoulder crossly. "Of course I must help you. 'Twas I who put you into this mess. I only said it would be difficult."

"Is there a long window or a balcony at the house?" asked Eleanor intently. "Think, Orlando. You know the house. I don't."

"Good Lord, I don't know. I didn't— Wait a minute, I think there is as I remember. A balcony at the side of the house."

Eleanor thought for a long moment, then began, "It is

the most vexing thing, for there is a fête at Mrs. Beaumont's house tonight. We can do nothing until after that. I shall have to plead a headache to get home early. At about one o'clock I shall begin to complain of it, so that we must come home early. You shall place yourself beneath my window at about half past three, for then, hopefully, all the servants will have gone to bed. I shall leave a candle in the window so you know which it is. And, Mr. Fairfax, you must bring with you"—she sat and thought again for several moments—"you must bring with you certain pieces of equipment: foremost, a long length of stout rope, so that I may let myself out from the window, for I cannot chance Cecy or Hartley hearing me on the stairs. You will either have to climb up to give it to me or throw it up."

Mr. Fairfax thought the rope would present few problems, nor was he too dismayed when she demanded that he bring with him something to force the window with, though he was not quite certain where he could lay his hands on such an instrument. He was, however, entirely unprepared and quite as dismayed when she named her third requirement.

"And then I must needs have some men's clothing!" said Eleanor, unabashed. "I'll never be able to climb in skirts."

"Miss Needwood! You cannot possibly dress in men's clothes. Suppose someone recognizes you! Think of your reputation!"

"If someone recognizes me at that time in the morning, my reputation is ruined anyway," Eleanor pointed out reasonably. "But it'll be more obvious I'm a female if I'm in skirts. Bring me a cloak and I can keep my face hidden."

"I think you must be mad, Miss Needwood."

"Very likely," said Eleanor dryly. "But if we get caught, you can always marry me and save my tarnished name! Now, remember, Orlando, I rely on you."

CHAPTER
18

Mrs. Beaumont's fête was one of the season's great events, and by midnight, when Lady Cecily's party entered the house in Portman Square, it was already crowded.

Mrs. Beaumont, their hostess, was quite a character. Reputed to have been of low origin, she had inherited vast estates in the north. Having married a colonel of militia who became a member for the county where her large estates lay, she had in recent years become one of fashions' leaders. Her style of living was luxurious and full of ostentation. Her preference for a nobleman before a titleless gentleman was shown in a manner so ridiculously wanting in tact and good sense that she offended innumerable people. Nonetheless, her fêtes were thronged with the *grand monde*, and her system of excluding all but persons of rank entirely amused the fashionable world, especially when they saw a man of talent or fortune, whom others admired, refused entree to her salons.

As Cecily's guest, Eleanor had received no such rebuff, but she entered the house without much hope of enjoyment, not knowing if Markham was coming, but assuming that anyway he would be in Lady Hervey's train.

Mrs. Beaumont met them effusively at the top of the stairs, which had Cecily digging Eleanor in the ribs with glee, since she, too, shared society's equivocal feelings about the odious woman, so steeped in self-esteem. But Eleanor could not share her impish delight as she would probably usually have done. On the contrary, her heart was full of misgivings and she was thoroughly depressed. Everything seemed to have gone wrong: that dreadful rumor, her argument with Markham, and now, worst of all, the unspeakable painting. She hardly knew where to turn. She had had a wild desire to cry on Cecily's shoulder and tell her all about it, only Cecily would be sure to tell her brother. She could not bear it were Markham ever to find out. It was bad enough that he already despised her.

She suddenly thought she saw Lord Markham at the other end of the ballroom and turned quickly away lest he should think she was searching for him. She wished she could control the sudden quickening inside and steeled herself to receive unmoved the coldly correct half bow or cut direct that had been her lot in recent days.

She herself was attended as ever by Lord Veren, and she knew that Mr. Hervey would certainly wait on her when he arrived, much as usual. The thought gave her no comfort, for she could certainly not allow things to go on as they were much longer, since tongues were already wagging preposterously. Some people were already saying she was fast, and that boded ill if she was ever to find herself a suitable husband in that elite company. She was particularly worried about the marquess.

Amusing as was Mr. Hervey, he had no serious intentions and could take care of himself. But Veren posed a real problem. Her second refusal to become his marchioness had but whet his appetite, and he was as much her slave as ever. Indeed, he had that very evening come with a message from his sister that desired her company at a house party, an invitation she would be at some difficulty in refusing. Yet refuse she must. It was too bad of her to keep someone as nice as Lord Veren dangling. She would simply have to make him turn his attentions elsewhere.

The future seemed so grim, she could not help it showing on her face. For a brief moment her eyes and mouth displayed her misery for all to see, and when Lord Markham, who had watched her since her entry from the comparative concealment of a small embrasure, saw her suddenly recollect herself and put on a dazzling smile for the assembly, it went to his heart. Unaccountably he walked straight across the ballroom to stand before her. He bit the inside of his cheek, as if amused at himself, his face assuming an ironic expression, then firmly said, "Dance with me, Eleanor," holding out his hand while ignoring completely the friends who stood around.

It was quite impossible. She was engaged to dance the first set with the marquess. He was but that moment fetching her a cordial. Without knowing what she did, Eleanor held out her hand to him and found herself walking with him into the set forming for the cotillion.

Eleanor could neither look at Markham nor, for a few moments, could she speak. He watched her pretending to be careless, looking with feigned interest all around her, but he sensed her cares.

"What's wrong, Eleanor?" he said.

"Wrong? What could be wrong?" Eleanor replied lightly. She threw him her glittering smile. "I was half afraid I wouldn't be thought fine enough for Mrs. Beaumont," she said gaily, "but she decided I wasn't *too* low to grace her rooms."

"Good God! I should think not! Odious woman—but something is wrong. What has upset you?"

Taking this as a cue and remembering what was ahead of her later, she put her fingers to her forehead, saying with a sigh, "I have a sick headache a little, sir. Indeed, I think it begins to get worse."

"A headache? Poor Eleanor. Perhaps later you will tell me what is really wrong?"

Her brow clouded. "Nothing is wrong," she said indignantly. "Why should I not have a headache?"

"No reason in the world that I can think of. But you haven't."

"If you have come only to quarrel with me, I don't know why you have asked me to dance," said Eleanor pettishly. "I quite thought we were agreed that we need not be seen together any longer. My credit is quite good enough now for you not to need to waste your time on me."

"Your credit may be good, but your tongue still needs the edge dulled," he replied wryly.

"Miss Hervey doubtless is more to your taste," Eleanor murmured sweetly.

"You are behindhand with your gossip, Miss Needwood," he informed her. "Miss Hervey has lately been seen with Mr. Fairfax."

"Mr. Fairfax!" In view of her recent interview with that gentleman and the plans they had made together earlier, Eleanor could not prevent a heightened color, which Lord Markham was quick to notice and which confused him.

"Now, why should *that* upset you, Eleanor?" he mused. "Of all your many admirers, I had quite thought him to be off the field."

"*All* my admirers? You are too kind, Lord Markham," said Eleanor. "Especially as we both know you don't mean it."

"How can you say such a thing? I was one of your first admirers, remember?"

"But not one of my last. That I *do* remember. Lowering indeed to be . . . to be the *last* woman in the world that you would wish to . . . after our friendship. The very last . . ." She made a valiant attempt to keep her voice spirited, but it faltered unaccountably, and she could not continue.

The dance had brought them very close. Their hands were held fast. Their eyes locked, and he saw that hers swam in unshed tears. "Ah, no, Eleanor. Don't. I never meant you to overhear that. I was in a vile temper. You made me mad as fire with Veren. Say that this business has not made it impossible for us to be . . . friends."

His gentle tone surprised her. A delicate blush painted her cheeks, and she turned her eyes aside, blinking away her tears, not enough sure of him to wear her heart upon her sleeve. Making a great effort to control her voice, which would shake absurdly, she replied, apparently amused, "Oh, I think not. You are much too important to my good name for me to do without you, my lord. Besides, I got my own back by telling you off so roundly, didn't I?"

"You did!" said Markham wryly as she withdrew her hand. "Trust you not to pander to my self-esteem."

"You don't need *me* for that, surely?" asked Eleanor sweetly.

"You vixen!" he exclaimed with a wry laugh. "I suppose it is those sweet little remarks that have made our friendship so precious to me."

Her mouth twitched at the corners, and she flicked open her fan to cover it. "La, sir," she replied modestly. "Are you trying to turn the head of a simple country girl?"

"I try to give provincials every consideration," he replied, taking up her tone and enjoying her company much as usual.

"Ah, but when I am with you, sir, I am not a provincial," she reminded him.

"But you are still a troublesome woman! And you have yet to tell me what is worrying you. Shall you tell me now?"

Just as earlier she longed to tell Cecily, so she had another overwhelming urge to tell him all about it; indeed, she was absolutely on the verge of it when into her mind sprang a mad vision that had been there on and off since the afternoon. It was a vision, wildly distorted, of a painting. In it she could just about recognize her own features, but they were attached to a mountain of female flesh lying provocatively across purple silk on a well-known divan. She closed her eyes, opened them again quickly, and threw him another brilliant smile. "You are imagining it, sir."

Lord Markham sighed heavily. "Ah, well, if you won't tell me, I cannot make you. But remember that we have resumed our friendship, won't you? If you do think of anything you wish to tell me, I shall always be at your service."

"You are too good, but I don't expect it."

He shrugged, then seeing that a number of gentlemen were clearly waiting on the periphery to ask Eleanor to take the floor, he said, "At least you'll save me another dance? You can tell me then if something has occurred to you."

The thought of having to bear another cross-examination did not appeal to Eleanor. She said quite casually, "Better perhaps content ourselves with this one, my lord. We don't want all that talk starting up again, do we?" she said demurely.

"I have no objection whatever to people talking, Eleanor. You must save me another," he said firmly.

She was spared the need to answer him by having to walk to the end of the set. The agitation his words had caused had time to subside by the time she joined him again.

Markham, too, walked the length of the set, and as he did so his eye fell again on the Marquess of Veren waiting patiently at the side to claim his partner.

"You know, Eleanor, I hope you are not building up too much store by Veren," he said as they met up again. "He's the best of good fellows, but he's known to be one for the ladies."

"Oh! Do you think he's only flirting with me, my lord," said Eleanor, rallying. "Well, you should know for a certainty."

Markham did not notice her irony. "There have been any number of girls singled out by him, and it has all led to nothing."

"So you have said. That seems to be the case with a good many men in town," she observed dryly.

"What I am saying, Eleanor, is that if anything he has said has led you to believe he will propose, do not depend on it. I do not hesitate to warn you, knowing how you are placed."

"You do not think he will propose, then?" asked Eleanor artlessly. "Mama will be disappointed. And his attentions have certainly been very marked."

"Poor Eleanor, you are still not quite up to snuff in these things. Veren has raised expectations as often as ... as often as ..."

"As often as *you* have, no doubt," said Eleanor with a cheerful smile. "I think I understand you only too well, my lord, and I thank you for your warning. Thank goodness you have told me, for here he comes now. I think he is going to claim his partner at last!"

And indeed the Marquess of Veren did that very moment come to demand of Lord Markham that he give up Miss Eleanor, whom he had so shamefully stolen!

Lord Markham could not help noticing the friendliness of Eleanor's greeting to the marquess. As he stood at the side of the ballroom with his arms folded, more than one of the gossips commented that Lord Markham appeared to have returned to the chase in the matter of "that young lady."

Cecily, too, had been closely watching her brother dancing with Eleanor. When he had so calmly taken her from under Veren's nose after not noticing her for so long, she had thought that things must finally have come to a head, but now that he had so tamely released her, she knew not what to make of it.

"Ah, there you are, brother," she said, coming up beside him. "How glad I am to see you and Nell speaking again. I see that you are watching her with Veren. I am always struck by what a handsome couple they make."

"I wish you would not foster such hopes in Eleanor's breast," her brother replied impatiently. "You know what Veren is. I should not wish to see Eleanor made miserable."

"Miserable, my love? Why should she be miserable?"

"You do not take your duties as chaperone seriously enough, Cecy," said her brother irritably. "You should warn her off when a man has a certain reputation."

"Brother, do you think that Veren is amusing himself with Miss Needwood?"

"I fear it, Cecy," he said heavily. "You know how often he has encouraged similar expectations."

"I see it quite differently, Markham. Which is why I have viewed the increasing friendship between Eleanor and the marquess with a good deal of pleasure. It would be a *great* match for her. Even her stepmama could not be displeased! And he has gone about it in quite the most unexceptionable way."

"It is a great deal too bad of you to be encouraging her in such ambitions. I doubt he means anything by it."

"On the contrary. He means everything! He has already proposed to Eleanor."

At first Markham did not take in his sister's words, but when they had indeed sunk in, he turned to face her with such an incredulous look on his face as quite shocked the Lady Cecily.

"Are you telling me that Veren has proposed to Eleanor, Cecy, and you did not even bother to tell me?" he asked indignantly.

"What had it to do with you, brother?" asked Cecily innocently.

"You know what people have been saying about us."

"I do, dearest, and it is a good deal too bad of them. And they will see how wrong they have been when she marries Veren."

This did not seem to give Lord Markham any comfort.

"You say he has proposed to Eleanor, are you certain?"

"Yes, dear. Quite certain. Indeed, I even overheard him the second time. They didn't realize, but I was in the arbor nearby and he thought they were—"

"The second time? The second time? Do you mean she refused him the first time?" Markham asked eagerly.

"Yes, and the second, too, though that was going a bit far. A man will always ask twice, but three times . . ."

"One might even think that she doesn't mean to have him," Markham pointed out in a sudden burst of good humor.

"I cannot believe that, Markham, when the alternative is Sir Maltby Tweede!"

"One alternative, certainly," said Markham, moving away.

It was his intention to find out Eleanor again. If nothing else, his sister's words had shown him something of his own heart. He was feeling absurdly cheerful. Seeing her in a distant part of the room still dancing with Veren, he began to jostle his way through the crowd to reach her. His progress was slowed by a hand on his shoulder. Turning, he found himself side by side with Francis Hervey.

"What, you here?" said Markham, surprised to see him. "I shouldn't have expected to find you at the Beaumonts."

"Oh, it has its attractions, don't you know?" replied Francis, inclining his head toward the end of the hall, where Eleanor was now surrounded by a small crowd.

They eyed each other like two stags in a rutting season. Rather than allow him a chance to get near to Eleanor, Markham even preferred to give up his own opportunity.

"This is a dashed bore, Francis," he said casually. "What about a hand or two of piquet? They've a neat little setup in that little octagonal room near the door."

Francis noted that Markham glanced back at Eleanor as they went. There was an astute expression on his face. When they had settled themselves down and were picking up their cards, he said quietly, "Why didn't you tell me you were serious about Miss Needwood, blockhead?"

Lord Markham made no reply.

"You must know I'd never have chased after her if I'd known?"

"I didn't know myself then," said Markham. "Indeed, I begin to think myself the greatest of fools."

"You've always been that, old fellow," said Francis with a cheeky grin.

"I'm glad we haven't to fall out about her, at any rate, Francis. I never knew what you felt about her. You've been seen hanging on to her skirts enough."

"Of course I have. She's a pearl without price. Irresistible," said Francis, choosing his words carefully.

"But you know me. I'm not ready for all that orange-blossom-and-bridesmaid stuff. A bit too hot for me, old friend. I'll withdraw quietly now, like the sterling fellow I am, and leave the field to you. Mark you, I can't say as much for everyone, for I hear they're laying odds on Veren making an offer before the month's out."

Lord Markham touched the side of his nose conspiratorially. "I have it on the best authority he's done so already," he confided.

"Which authority?" asked Francis, frankly doubtful.

"Cecy."

"Oh, well, if Cecy says so, it must be true, for she's the biggest busybody I know. So Veren's proposed, has he? Phew—that's a deal of competition."

"Cecy says he offered twice and she refused him," said Markham, looking a trifle complacent.

"Twice! Good heavens. She *has* done well for herself. Mind, he's not the only interested party, they say. The old tabbies have been putting forward any number of names. They say that Holbrook has even been in the running, and he's as rich as Croesus. If I were you, I'd settle with her as soon as you can, for there's plenty of others willing to take her on if you don't. Young Fairfax is another, I'm told."

Markham laughed. "The ladies in *your* family are obviously not as busy as my sister, if you are still thinking of that one," he told him. "You are certainly behindhand. I rather think it's Letty he's chasing now."

"Letty! Good Lord! I wonder what Mother'll say to that?"

"Shouldn't see how she could possibly object myself," said Markham, suddenly generous to the young man whom, not a week before, he had referred to as a young whelp with the brain of a porcupine. "Good family, excellent fortune. Nothing wrong with him that a few years and a sensible wife won't cure."

Having given his friend something to think about, Markham decided to take his advice and went off in search of Eleanor. He was more than a little disappointed to hear that his sister's party had departed, Miss Needwood having had a headache. Determining that he would put his fate to the test first thing in the morning, he returned to the card room with Francis to make what he could of what had suddenly become a dull evening.

CHAPTER
19

Eleanor, after hearing the last of the servants go to bed, awaited her rendezvous with Mr. Fairfax. As ever, she puzzled, not about him, but about Lord Markham. She never knew what to make of him, never really knew what he thought of her. And it was infuriating that on the strength of what might mean nothing to him, he could stay away for so long and then, as soon as he lifted his finger, she had not been able to stop herself from dancing with him. And she had been unfair to Veren! Unfair! Unfair! When Veren had shown himself a real lover: deserving, amorous. He had never wavered in his devotion: a man whom all the world knew to be a great, a glorious match. Had she never met Markham, surely she'd have taken Veren? Mama would say that London had turned her head. Mama would probably say that Lord Veren was a mile too good for her! Mama would be *furious* if she found out that she had refused him! But then, Mama was always cross with her about something. Much more important was that Papa should never find out.

She could not think of Papa without imagining his mortification if that dreadful portrait ever became public property! Papa, who so clung to the proprieties.

Whose last warning had been that she should not get into any scrapes in London. What would he think if her name was bandied about as being the type of girl who would sit for such a . . . such a *thing* as that! Her hands flew to her cheeks, which became suddenly flooded with warmth when she remembered that he would be scarcely more shocked than Lord Markham. She could not help remembering that Cecily had so often referred to her parents as prudes. If his father was a prude, Lord Markham was probably the same. It ran in families! He would never speak to her again. Her eyes closed and she covered them with her hand. It would kill her if Markham were to learn of that painting.

There was a noise at the window which she only half heard and was still trying to identify, when another, sharper rap told her that Mr. Fairfax had come through the garden door and was now throwing up pebbles to attract her attention as arranged. She was over at the window in a flash, and Mr. Fairfax dropped a third stone he was about to lob up. She saw, with approval, that he had a length of rope at his feet and that he carried some clothes on one arm.

Eleanor opened the window and hissed at him, "Throw the rope up first!"

So careful was she not to make too much noise that she was obliged to repeat herself before he heard her, and her patience was wearing very thin when he threw the rope up six times before it had come anywhere near the vicinity of her window. What a booby with whom to share an adventure! Each time he missed, the rope clattered noisily to the ground.

She said sharply, "Throw it more carefully, or you'll waken the whole house."

"I'm doing my best. It isn't that easy," he snapped back, but this time the rope reached. She pulled the end into the room and tied it securely to the bedpost.

"Orlando!" she whispered. "Tie the clothes to the other end!"

This proved more difficult than it sounded. Mr. Fairfax first tried to tie all the clothes, including a large evening cloak and a light pair of evening pumps, in a single parcel and send it up. Halfway up, this loosened and fell down, enveloping him in clothing, much to Eleanor's amusement.

They were painstakingly obliged to send each piece of clothing up separately, and then Eleanor dressed up, thanking heaven she was tall, for they were really an acceptable fit if one did not look too closely. She blew out her candle and went back to the window. All seemed to be going well. In a few hours, God granted, she'd have that painting back and could destroy it. It was then that Mr. Fairfax ordered, "Now then, Eleanor, hold the rope and climb out onto the windowsill."

It seemed such a simple instruction! She was sure that when she was a little girl she'd have been able to do it without a qualm. Unaccountably, when she tried to do it now, her mouth went dry. She looked down to the garden below, and it seemed an inordinately long way.

"I'm sorry, Orlando," she was obliged to admit. "I can't!"

"What do you mean, you can't?" Orlando asked indignantly. "You mean you've got me here with all this stuff and you can't come down a simple rope! Well, if that isn't typical. When I've done all this!"

"Don't shout at me! It isn't my fault! And you'll waken everybody!"

"I don't see it makes much difference if you can't get down a simple rope!"

"Well, I can't. You'll have to come up and help me down."

"Help you? How can I do that? I'm not Hercules."

"I think I *knew* that," Eleanor said with heavy irony.

"Good Lord! What an ingrate you are. I needn't be here, you know! I could be out enjoying myself."

"Yes, you might, had you been more of a gentleman and not painted that disgraceful picture!"

"You're exaggerating. It isn't anything like as bad as you make out!"

"When I see it I'll tell you if I agree with you," she replied acidly. "Now, come up this rope and help me down. I am sure that I'll be able to do it if I know you are just below me."

Having enjoined her to check the rope to see that the knot was secure, Mr. Fairfax climbed slowly up the rope and sat himself on the windowsill, puffing when he got there. "I'm sure you might do it easily if you tried," he said kindly, climbing across the sill into the room. "Really, there's nothing to it." Then he chanced to look at Eleanor. "I say!" he exclaimed, going red in the face. "Are you sure you want to go out like that? It's a bit . . . a bit . . ."

"Don't you *dare* say anything," cried Eleanor, seeing his undisguised astonishment, for she, too, had been shocked at her appearance in the mirror, not having suspected how evening breeches would so accentuate the contours of her limbs. "It's all your fault that I've got to go through with this fiasco."

Mr. Fairfax hastened to reassure her, but getting more and more tangled in his words was finally shamed into

207

silence, and without another word edged himself across the windowsill, hanging by the rope just below it.

Eleanor took a deep breath, drew the evening cloak closely about her, and sat on the windowsill, letting her feet in the male evening pumps, too loose for her, dangle. She grasped the rope in one hand, and then, turning around so that the front of her body pressed closely against the window ledge, she began to edge her way down. Orlando was just below her, and as she slipped nervously across the sill and down the wall, her foot felt for and found something to steady it.

"Take it easy. That's my ear!" cried Fairfax indignantly.

But Eleanor was past being able to control her movements. She had that moment looked down and seen that the garden was a very long way down. Frantically she grasped at the rope, felt herself slipping, and kicked out erratically. This time her heel found Orlando's hand, and before he realized what was happening, she had barked his knuckles with her shoe and he'd loosed his fingers and felt himself falling to the ground, his descent being halted by a large, spiky bush.

Eleanor, meanwhile, clung on to the rope and, scarcely daring to move, asked, "Are you all right?"

There was no immediate answer, and when she heard a groaning sound from below, she repeated urgently, "Orlando! Are you all right?"

"What do you think?" he said, aggrieved. "This bush is prickly. Deuced prickly!"

Despite her own predicament, Eleanor could not help giggling. "You'll have to climb up again, Orlando," she whispered. "I'm stuck."

"Indeed? Climb up again, Orlando. Just let me stick

my toe in your ear, Orlando. Oh, and if you haven't suffered enough, Orlando, let me tread on your fingers again, Orlando!"

"Don't be such a baby. We've got too much to do."

Cautiously Orlando eased himself out of the bush, groaning at every spike, but when he put one of his feet to the floor, his leg crumpled beneath him. Eleanor heard his moan and called out frantically, "What's wrong?"

"It's my foot. I think ..." Another long moan, and she saw him clutch his leg and fall to the ground. "I think ... I've ... broken it."

There was a moment of silence as the magnitude of the tragedy struck them both. Then, without warning, the door to the garden through which Orlando had earlier entered swung ajar to reveal, in the light from the street lantern outside, the figure of Lord Markham.

CHAPTER

20

It took but a moment for him to take in the interesting scene before him. His glance moved from Mr. Fairfax at his feet to Miss Needwood stuck at the top of the rope just underneath the window, and putting his hand on his heart, he said, " 'But soft! What light through yonder window breaks? It is the east.' And— Eleanor is the sun." Then, looking down at Orlando, he said contritely, "Oh, I'm sorry. That's your line, isn't it?"

Mortified to be found in such a position by one whom he had begun to think of as his greatest adversary, Mr. Fairfax scrambled to his feet, then, groaning hugely, fell down again, his face so pale that it looked positively green in the moonlight.

"Oh, you poor old fellow," said Markham at once, getting down on his knee beside him. "Let me look at it." Then, a moment later, he added "Yes, it's a break all right. Don't for goodness' sake try to move. I'll get you some help."

There was a movement from above and a slight cough. "I don't know if you two have noticed," Eleanor put in impatiently, "but I'm stuck up here."

Lord Markham looked up and saw at once that in

spite of her pretense at just being cross, Eleanor was really quite scared.

He was over at the wall in a moment, whispering to Fairfax to "hang on, there's a good fellow."

Shinning up the rope, he reached to beneath Eleanor and told her to rest her feet on his shoulders, which she gratefully did.

"Now then, Eleanor, if you can only reach up one hand at a time, we can get you back inside."

"I can't!" whispered Eleanor fearfully.

"Don't be silly. Of course you can, I'm just below you, and I'll move up with you. Keep your feet on my shoulders and you can't fall."

"I can't," whispered Eleanor more urgently, and Markham heard the terror in her voice.

"It's all right, sweetheart," he said softly. "I'll not let you fall. Just stay still and we'll think what to do."

So terrified was Eleanor that she didn't even hear the endearment.

"Now then, dearest, hold still," Markham said gently. "I'm pulling you down so that I can hold you."

"No! I can't," insisted Eleanor, still aware of the need not to be overheard.

"I'm here, Eleanor, stretch your arm out to me."

Eleanor looked down again, shuddered, and then blindly held out an arm, which Markham grabbed and pulled around his neck.

"Good girl! Now the other one," he said quietly.

Almost without thinking she stuck her arm into space and Markham grasped it, bringing it around his neck and pulling her body so that it intertwined with his own.

Eleanor felt instinctively for safety, and for several moments clung thankfully, the length of her body against Markham's. Her breath came fast, and as he felt her in his arms for the first time, his breath began to come as fast. Through her fear she realized how improper was her situation, and despite her wishes went to draw away. Lord Markham drew her to him again. "Don't be silly, Eleanor," he said shortly, "this is no time to be thinking about the proprieties. Keep your arms around my neck and hold on to me."

Before she knew what had happened, he had lowered them both to the bottom of the rope. So terrified was she that it was some moments before Eleanor realized she was down, and she continued to cling to Lord Markham, who was in no hurry to release her. A groan from nearby Mr. Fairfax brought her back to reality, and Eleanor pulled away.

"Orlando," she whispered urgently. "Are you all right?"

"I think he's broken his foot," Markham interposed. "But whatever he's done, he can't stand on it."

"What can we do?" said Eleanor, dismayed.

Lord Markham eyed them both with a rather quizzical look. "I'm not by any chance helping at an elopement, am I?" he said politely. "Or is it a masquerade," he continued, running his eyes over Eleanor's shapely limbs.

"Good Lord, no!" said Fairfax, hastening to reassure him. "I'll tell you how it is, man, if you'll just—"

"Don't dare to tell him," interrupted Eleanor, urgently pulling her cloak closely around herself. "I don't wish him to know! And what are you doing here, anyway?"

"As well for you that I *was* walking past, I'd say," said Markham, amused.

"He's right, Eleanor. Let him help. I can't now that I've got this dratted foot, and someone must."

"Why? I am perfectly well able to deal with it on my own."

"Do you know how to get to—"

"I shall take a chair," she broke in haughtily.

"And what shall you do when you get there? You couldn't even manage to climb down a rope," he reminded her.

"No matter," she said firmly. "I shall not have it bandied about. I'm certain I shall manage."

"Would someone mind telling me what we are talking about," interposed Markham with maddening deliberation.

"Nothing to do with you," said Eleanor.

"Oh! I'll go, then, shall I? You'll manage to climb up, will you? Or aren't you going up again?"

"Don't be a fool, Eleanor. We'll have to tell him," said Orlando impatiently, for Markham had begun to turn away. "It's the painting, Markham. We've got to get it back!"

Markham's attention was engaged at once. "Painting? What painting?"

Eleanor stamped her foot. "I won't have you tell him, Orlando, do you hear? I won't!"

"Have you got yourself into a scrape, Eleanor?" Markham asked severely. "Best tell me if you have."

"No! *I* haven't got *myself* into a scrape," said Eleanor, coming increasingly to realize that Markham was going to find out about the painting whatever she did.

"This ... this ... idiot has got me into a scrape, and now he hasn't even the ... grace to keep it to himself!"

By now she'd all but lost control of herself, and when she heard Markham and Fairfax whisper simultaneously, "Shh!" she stormed away into a dark corner of the garden, mouthing through clenched teeth, "Urgggh!" which came out oddly strangulated.

"She has every right to be angry, I suppose," Fairfax admitted, "after what I've done."

"And still I'm kept in the dark—quite literally," Markham reminded him.

"I painted a portrait of Eleanor, you see."

"As all the world knows. But what of it?"

"No, not that one ... another one."

Lord Markham pricked up his ears at that. "Another? Why? When? I hadn't heard that Eleanor sat for two portraits."

"She didn't. I used my imagination!"

"Imagination?" snapped Eleanor bitterly, "Pure invention, rather."

"I ... see," said Markham, catching on. "You painted a portrait of Eleanor using your imagination. But what of it? Why all the fuss?"

"It's ... it's ... the kind of painting it *is*," said Eleanor, becoming more tangled in every word.

Lord Markham suddenly became a good deal less sociable. Standing over Mr. Fairfax, he said with every trace of humor gone from his voice, "Exactly *what* kind of painting did you execute of Miss Needwood, Mr. Fairfax? I am most interested."

Orlando tugged at his neckcloth, feeling suddenly quite nervous. "Miss Needwood makes too much of it," he hastened to reassure him. "The merest hint of ...

well, not even that really, just a slight tone of . . . nothing offensive . . . and quite hidden in draperies." He staggered through his recital, ending lamely with, "And I'd never have done so but for Lady Pelham."

Lord Markham had taken a step nearer to Fairfax, when the mention of that lady stopped him.

"Violet Pelham? What's she in all this?" he said, confused.

"She suggested I paint a portrait of Miss Needwood without . . . well, disrobed . . . though," he hastened to reassure him, "I didn't, of course, only a slight suggestion of . . . and now she's had it stolen!"

"You little worm," said Markham in disgust. "If you weren't already lying on the floor, I'd knock you there."

"No, no! You mistake! It's nothing like so bad . . ."

Lord Markham examined his fingernails. "Tell me, Fairfax," he said mildly, "would you paint Miss Hervey like it?"

At his words, Mr. Fairfax stared miserably at the ground, wordless.

"I see," said Markham, dangerously quiet. "I'd like to slit your throat, you curst commoner. And to blame it on Violet Pelham—"

"But it's true! I'd never have thought of painting it but for her!" cried Fairfax, incensed into speech by Markham's unfairness. "And now she's taken it to do heaven knows what mischief with, so we've got to get it back."

"And what made her think up so disgusting a plan, do you think, my lord?" asked Eleanor, facing him, eyes blazing, for to hear him defend Lady Pelham at such a time was just about the last straw.

"I haven't the vaguest notion," he said carelessly, adding, "if she *did* do it."

"Of course she did it!" said Eleanor, wishing she could scream at him instead of having to hiss at him in this absurd manner. "To get back at you!"

"Oh, I might have known I'd be to blame for any scrapes you got yourself into, Eleanor. And just how would it get back at me?"

"You know very well! Everyone knows you and she were thick as thieves a few months ago," she carelessly.

"Oh? Do they?" he said, an amused look showing in the corners of his eyes and mouth.

"Yes, they do!" Eleanor affirmed tartly. "She probably heard these ridiculous rumors of an attachment between us and intended to make you look a fool for . . . running after someone who would . . . would sit for such a painting! Though why she would believe such an absurd rumor, when it is obvious that your taste runs to far . . . far *riper* women. And why she had to pick on me I am not in a position to say, not having that lady's confidence!"

To Eleanor's dismay, she felt the tears welling in her eyes and searched in vain for a handkerchief in the pockets of her borrowed coat. Lord Markham pulled a handkerchief from his own pocket and obligingly gave it to her. While she was dabbing at her eyes he said quietly so only she could hear, "Don't talk such nonsense, Eleanor. You know exactly in which direction my taste in women is running."

"Don't you dare to flirt with me at such a time," she said crossly.

"No, perhaps it is not quite the right time," he agreed

216

suavely, looking her over. "Perhaps I had better wait until you look rather more the part. It's a little like flirting with one's younger brother!"

"Oh! If that isn't like you!"

He stepped back and looked her up and down very deliberately. "But not very like you, I fear," he said with a wry smile. "Whatever made you think you could get away with being a man?"

"I had no choice," she explained, turning red. "I couldn't very well go about the streets with Mr. Fairfax, dressed in my ball gown. And I have to get back that painting. I'll be ruined else. It would kill my father if he thought I'd sat for such a . . . such a . . ."

With every word, Markham could see the panic in her eyes grow. Breaking in on her, he said calmly, "Will you let me help you get it?"

"What? You?"

"You plainly think it is largely my fault." He smiled a brief, winning little smile. "My indefatigable charm leading the lady to unmentionable lengths apparently! And don't you always say that I never do anything for anybody?"

"You don't."

"Then let me help you in this. If she has it, we'll get it back."

"You want only to see it!" she scoffed.

"I want to make sure no one else does," he insisted.

"I don't want *you* to see it!" she said, showing her distress.

"I'll close my eyes," he murmured, raising a hand to hide his smile at her indignation.

"You think this is funny, don't you," challenged Eleanor indignantly.

"Of course I don't," he assured her, taking hold of her hands. "But you did rather bring it on yourself. I told you not to sit for Fairfax."

"Ooh! When it was all your fault that I sat for him at all. I'd never have done so had you not made me angry."

"Yes, I rather thought that was why you insisted on doing it. And since you blame me, you'll let me help, won't you?"

"I don't see that you have a choice," Orlando suggested urgently. "I won't be fit for ages with this leg, and the longer *she* has it, the more people she can show it to."

Eleanor's eyes darted here and there all about her as if seeking inspiration for any other plan that might present itself, but for once her fertile imagination let her down. "Do you think we shall be able to find it?" she asked at length. "We shall have to break in, you know."

"I think I'd realized that," said Markham. "But at least I know the house well, so that should help us."

"Of course you do!" said Eleanor acidly. "How fortunate. Indeed, I can't think how I came to attempt it without your particular expertise."

Markham ignored her, saying only, "There's a little balcony at the side of the house that will not only give us an easy way in, but which leads into a small salon on the first floor. From there it is only a step to Lady Pelham's dressing room, and if the painting is not there, it'll be in her bedroom next door, for sure. With a bit of luck it'll take only minutes to find it."

"Suppose she should wake up?" said Eleanor fearfully.

"Then, my dear girl, we are in the soup."

CHAPTER

21

Having deposited Orlando in a hackney carriage and sent him home, Markham and Eleanor made their way cautiously to Jermyn Street. Once or twice they passed other night saunterers, and each time Eleanor pulled her cloak so closely around her that Markham finally said, "For God's sake, Eleanor, do you want to tell everyone you're not a man? Just act naturally and keep your hat well over your eyes. Anyone we meet at this time of night will be so fuddled, they'll never realize what you are."

Lady Violet's house was on the corner of Jermyn and Duke streets. A street lamp glowed brightly in front of the house, and as they walked around to the side street, out of its telling glow, where a long brick wall noted the perimeter of the property, they noticed a little balcony. Leaving Eleanor on guard in the shadow of a plane tree by the roadside, Markham shinned up the wall and balanced precariously on top. Taking a grip of the corner of the house, he leaned across and grasped the railings of the balcony with his other hand. Letting go of the wall and grabbing another rail, he scrambled up over the balcony. The long windows were secured only by a latch, and since Markham had brought with him

Orlando's knife, it was a moment's work for him to gain access.

Waving to Eleanor, Markham disappeared inside the house.

Left on guard, Eleanor was getting extremely anxious. She had never been out on her own at night and was horrified by the number of people still out and about. She even saw friends of Cecily's descending from their carriage to enter a house farther down the street, having obviously just returned late from Mrs. Beaumont's fête! It was a nerve-racking business altogether, and each time anyone passed, thankfully all of them on the other side of the street, Eleanor shrank back into the shadows.

Markham was sure the painting would be found in Lady Violet's dressing room. Taking off his evening pumps, he crept silently along the hall and entered the little room that led to Violet's bedroom. There was not a sound to be heard from anywhere else in the house, but when he had closed the dressing room door behind him, he heard voices emanating from the lady's bedchamber! The shock brought him up sharp, and he stood as if frozen just inside the dressing room door, listening hard. Clearly the candles were still lit, for he could see a glow of light spreading along the bottom of the door. He cursed, remembering the heavy curtains in Violet's bedroom, which must have stopped them from seeing the light. Hardly daring to breathe, he moved silently over to the door, but all of a sudden a huge grin lit his features. Voices were indeed coming from the next room, one very well known to him, speaking and laughing in the seductive low tones he remembered so well, the other clearly male. He remembered that society had recently been buzzing with tales of the lady's new conquest, and grinned again, even more widely. So, she really did have Lord James FitzSimmons in her thrall! You had to hand it to her, thought Markham. She really was a *one*.

It was unnecessary now to be quite so careful, and to his silent satisfaction he soon found, stuffed behind a dressing cabinet, the unframed canvas. Pausing only to confirm, with an appreciative lift of his eyebrows, that it was indeed what he sought, he swiftly retraced his steps to the balcony.

He had been gone no more than five minutes, yet to Eleanor it had seemed an eternity. Her nerves were at the breaking point, and seeing a gentleman approaching, this time on her own side of the street, while every moment she expected Markham to reappear from the balcony, she panicked and ran around the corner.

Seeing the disappearing figure ahead and having heard of London footpads, the gentleman paused just beneath the balcony, uncertain whether to proceed.

It was at this moment that Markham, reappearing on the balcony and seeing a gentlemanly shape below in an evening cloak and hat, leaned over and whispered urgently, "Catch this!"

Looking up, the gentleman instinctively caught the canvas, then unrolled it.

Eleanor risked peeping around the corner and saw the whole episode. As the gentleman unraveled the canvas and held it up to look at it, his face was no longer in the shadow. His face thus revealed, Eleanor recognized it at once and cried out in horror, "Papa!"

Mr. Needwood allowed the canvas to roll up again and peered unbelievingly along the pavement. "Eleanor? Is that you?" He looked from her to the figure above and said winsomely, "My dear child, I wonder if you think I deserve an explanation."

"Markham! At last! My dear, I was never more shocked in my life!" said Cecily, throwing herself at him as Harrop tried to help him out of his coat.

"Wait a minute, Cec," said Markham repressively with a glance at her butler. "We'll go in there, shall we?"

But once in the salon, there was no stopping her. "This dreadful business!" she cried, chafing her hands together. "How could that vulgar little man have done that? To paint such a—"

"He's a fool," said Markham, dismissing him with a slighting gesture.

"She should have *told* me, not stolen off into the night like that," said Cecily wildly, quite unable to contain herself. "I'd have done *something*."

"Oh? What? You advised her not to sit for the other painting, as I understand it, and you were quite right, so you'd be the last person she'd tell. You know Miss Needwood."

"But to climb out of the window, Markham. She might have broken her neck. And in men's clothing!"

A pleasant little memory stirred in Lord Markham. He smiled briefly. "Yes, there's no denying she's got spirit."

"You can't possibly think it was sensible of her? Supposing she had been seen."

"As I remember, she *was* seen," her brother reminded her. "And by the last person in the world she would wish. Fancy Mr. Needwood deciding to come to town like that. And then to be walking around the streets at that time of night just because he couldn't get to sleep. Why couldn't he take some laudanum like anyone else! Phew, I tell you, it gave me a nasty turn to see him there. That's why I've been to call on Lady Pelham this morning instead of coming straight here. I thought that if I could only be in a position to reassure Mr. Needwood that this thing would go no further . . ."

"You've been to see that creature! After what she tried to do to Nell? Why on earth did you do that? I shouldn't have thought any friend of Nell's would ever wish to associate with her again."

"I don't want to *associate* with her, Cec, so you are not to be thinking any such thing. But I thought I'd better go there just the same, and I'll tell you why. When I had a chance to think properly, I realized that after all our efforts there was still nothing to prevent her from just *mentioning* the painting, even if we have managed to get it back from her. She'd know just how to use a choice snippet like that to do the most harm. I simply thought she should be made to see that it wasn't in her best interests."

"And just how did you manage that, pray?" said Cecily suspiciously. "Or is it best not to ask?"

"Cec, really!"

"Don't be sanctimonious, Markham. I know *men*. So how *did* you get her to agree to keep her mouth shut?"

"Oh, I had my methods."

"What methods?"

"I don't think I should tell you," said Markham maddeningly. "Women can't keep secrets. And I shouldn't like it to get around."

"Oh, a secret. She can have a secret about Nell, but

I'm not to be allowed to defend Nell with one about *her*!"

"Put like that, I suppose it *isn't* fair," Markham reflected. "Still, I don't intend to tell you all of it. But if I just say that when I went there last night, she was not entirely alone, you will understand some of it. . . ."

Cecily's eyes opened widely. "You mean she had a *man* with her? Who was it?"

"There! You see what I mean? You can't wait to find out, can you? And then you will tell all your friends and it will be all over town and I will no longer have my hold over her. Which is why I don't intend to tell you anything more."

"Well, it still doesn't seem fair to me. Why should she have an advantage over Nell?"

"I promise you, she hasn't. She knows that I should intervene should the slightest hint of such a painting ever leave her lips. My dear girl! Do you seriously think I should leave Miss Needwood's reputation to chance?"

Cecily had taken umbrage and didn't answer.

"And speaking of secrets," continued Lord Markham as if they were in complete accord, "I thought it as well to check on Fairfax, too, just to make sure he keeps his mouth shut, so I've been there as well. When I got there, little Letitia Hervey and his mother were waiting on him hand and foot on his bed of pain. I think it'll be a match there, by the way. Do you want to know what story that ninnyhammer is putting out about his foot? I promise you it'll divert you."

"It will have to be very funny to do that," said Cecily coldly.

"According to Letty, our hero was apparently walking along Bond Street, when a runaway horse pulling an elderly gentleman came flying past. He leapt from the pavement onto the carriage and managed to bring the horse under control. It was not until afterward that he realized he had broken his foot!"

Cecily broke into a trill of laughter. "Oh, no! How ridiculous! Our hero! How on earth did he think it up? And how did you manage to keep a straight face? I promise you, I shouldn't have."

"No, I don't suppose *you* would. Anyway, I managed, briefly, to get rid of the ladies and told him everything. I think you can be sure he won't ever mention the painting, because I reminded him that some wives look askance at episodes from their husband's pasts. I also told him that in my experience Letty was a little on the prudish side."

"That was clever."

"Yes, *I* thought so," he said smugly. "I thought that if I could only reassure Mr. Needwood that his daughter's reputation was safe, he might be less angry with her. I tell you, Cec, it gave me the devil of a start to see him there last night."

"I should rather think it *did*," said Cecily, wide-eyed. "He was mad as fire when he brought her here. Wanted to know what sort of chaperone I considered myself. And he said it in such a way, too. So quiet. So controlled. I was never so wretched in my life. I'd rather have one of Father's rakings down than go through that again. Though how he thinks I could have suspected such a plan, I don't know."

"Poor Cecy. It must have been the very devil. He scared the life out of me. Didn't raise his voice once, but I knew what he thought of me, all right."

"He can't have anything to blame *you* for, dearest. You only wanted to help her."

"Just the same . . . That's why I thought I'd get everything fixed up right and tight before I had to face him again. Where is Miss Needwood? Still asleep?"

"Asleep? La, brother. I thought you realized. No, but how could you, indeed? My dearest, the most vexing thing. Her father has taken her home."

"What? And you've been letting me run on all this time? What happened? What did he say?"

"He said that in the circumstances he thought it was quite the best thing for Eleanor to have a little quiet reflection at home. Oh, Markham, poor Nell. He said that he was . . . that he was shocked at what he had found in London and that he would never have allowed her to come at all had he realized that she would not be more carefully chaperoned, which is so unfair, when I have done everything one should! She has never been allowed to waltz, and when she wished to buy the dearest little bonnet in Bond Street the other day, I absolutely forbade her because Hart said it was a trifle roguish, and I would not take the chance! And, dearest, he said that, worst of all, she had been led into spending a huge amount of money which he could ill afford without any serious intention of finding a husband at all! He has a perfectly frightful old fogey of a friend who has apparently been writing all this while to tell him what Nell has been up to in London, which was what brought him to town in the first place, and the silly old fool told her father that Nell had refused Veren, which had him mad as fire! He said that Nell must have had her head turned by all the fuss made of her and that since she was ready to refuse unexceptionable offers like Veren's, she would obviously never marry."

At the end of this recital, Cecily sat heavily in a chair and began to cry into a little lace handkerchief.

"Poor Cec," said her brother, coming to put his arms around her. "What a dreadful time you have been having. It's all my fault. I shouldn't have asked you to chaperone her. I knew how headstrong she was."

Lady Cecily blew her nose briskly. "That's nonsense, Markham," she said at once. "You know how I adore Nell, and I've loved having her here, so you are not to be making out that I have not enjoyed it. I don't mind what her father says to me, it is Nell I am worried about. He'll incarcerate her at home now, and she'll never be seen again, and she's so beautiful, it isn't fair!" This last was said on a wail, and she buried her face in her handkerchief again.

"And what of Miss Needwood, Cec? How was she?"

"Stoical. But I could tell she was unhappy, brother. And you know that frightful stepmama will make her miserable at home. If only she could have taken Veren."

"Presumably she did not love him, Cec."

"Of course she did not, Markham, and you know perfectly well why she did not," replied his sister, coming out from her handkerchief.

There was an arrested look on Markham's face, and he took hold of his sister's hand urgently. "No, I don't. Tell me," he pressed.

"Oh, really, Markham! If you think I intend to pander to your vanity, you are mistaken."

"I don't want *that*, Cec, you know me better. It's just that I really need to be sure."

"Do you mean to tell me that you don't know how

she feels about you, Markham? Oh, really. You make me so cross. Why, the pair of you have been smelling of April and May for weeks, and you need to be *sure!*"

"You think she loves me, then?" he asked urgently, and there was such an incredulous look on his face that his sister was moved to kiss his cheek.

"Only you could be such a simpleton as to doubt it, dearest," she said with a smile. "Mama and I ordered our wedding hats an age ago."

"Best of sisters!" called Markham, letting her hand fall and walking briskly from the room into the hallway.

"But, Markham, where are you going?" she cried as she trailed after him.

"Where do you think I'm going? After them, of course!"

When Cecily's husband came in presently from seeing his man of affairs, she was seated at her dressing table, looking surprisingly cheerful after all the terrible events of the night.

"What are you looking so happy about, minx?" said her husband suspiciously. "I expected your chin to be on the floor now that your precious Markham isn't to marry Miss Needwood after all."

"That's all you know, Hart. Not marry Miss Needwood? I think, dearest, that rather than crowing, you had better be saving your money, since you will certainly owe me that pony any day now."

CHAPTER

22

Eleanor stared drearily from the window of her father's traveling chariot, noticing nothing she passed, scarcely believing it when her father declared that they were already at Newport Pagnell. She sighed and continued to gaze sightlessly, resting her chin on her knuckles.

"It's no use sighing, Nell," remonstrated her father mildly. "You must see that I had no choice but to fetch you home. I'd probably have done so even without that fracas last night after what I'd been hearing from my old friend."

"Fetch me home because Colonel Aspley told you I had some admirers, Father? Surely that is what I came to town to try to get?"

"You make light of it, girl, but people don't like it when young chits keep men dangling. This Veren, now. Why couldn't you have had him? From what Aspley tells me, he's young and with a good countenance. What was wrong with that? And you'd have had an opportunity to do the family some good as well. A wealthy man like that, and from a titled family. Who knows what you'd have been able to do for your sisters? I don't know what your mother'll say."

He felt her stiffen, and added more kindly, "There, there. You don't need to worry about that. I'll not let her bother you. And your sisters are wild to see you."

When she did not reply, he went on. "You'll find it a lot more comfortable at home, I'll warrant, Nell. It would never have done to have continued as we were, and I've told your mother so. That Maltby Tweede business, now. That's all at an end. You'll marry to please yourself, or not at all."

Still, Eleanor had nothing to say. "I can tell that you don't believe me, sweetheart, but you'll see," persevered Mr. Needwood. "Why, your mama doesn't even rail at me much for going to my greenhouses these days."

"Oh, Papa," said Eleanor, surprised into a smile. "How good you are to fret about me. I'm an ungrateful wretch."

"You've never been that, my dear. You just wait until you've got your own roof over your head, then you'll cheer up. I never liked the idea of you going to London. Who needs these town types? There's Clary Ingram, now. As straightforward a boy as you could hope for."

"I'll never marry Clary Ingram, Father," said Eleanor firmly.

"Oh! What, never?"

"No, Father," she said, softening the blow with a gentle squeeze of his hand.

"Oh, well," he said, returning the pressure. "Pity. I *like* the boy. But you can't tell what'll suit somebody else, I daresay."

He lapsed into a reverie. A few moments later he went on as if he hadn't interrupted his flow. "So, *not* Clary Ingram. And *not* Veren. Tell me, my dear, there isn't someone else you like, is there? Someone I should be expecting to hear from?"

She shook her head miserably, but even in the half light of the coach Mr. Needwood saw the spots of color pink her cheeks. He allowed the conversation to drop for several minutes, picking it up later by reflecting, "You know, Nell, I can't help thinking that I was a trifle unfair to Lord Markham."

He sensed her agitation and was emboldened to continue. "From what you tell me, he did nothing but try to get you out of a difficulty your own headstrong behavior placed you in. Of course, I wasn't to know that at the time, so I don't altogether blame myself. Any father would have acted as I did. But I should have given him a chance to explain. Yes, I certainly should have given him a chance to explain."

When she didn't reply, he said tentatively, "I'd better write to him and explain matters. Shall I, Nell? Apologize, you know. For jumping to conclusions. Express my sense of obligation to him, and to that sister of his. I can't help thinking I was a touch harsh there, too. After all, how could *she* be expected to know that young rascal would dare to paint such a—"

"Oh, sir," Eleanor broke in hurriedly, unwilling to bring on a return of the near apoplexy that had seized her father when he saw Fairfax's second painting of his daughter. "I do wish you *would* write to Cecily. She and Hartley have been so very, very kind to me. Cecily has treated me more like a sister than a friend. Indeed, sir, it is the greatest affliction to me that you were so cold to her."

"Like a sister, eh?" her father reflected. "Then I shall

certainly write to her and thank her for it. And what of young Markham, eh? Should I write to him as well?"

Again, in the half light he saw her color, but she only shrugged her shoulders, saying, "As you wish, Father." From which he drew his own conclusions.

They lapsed into silence, each in deep thought, as the milestones passed. Mr. Needwood, in his corner, gently dozed off, while his daughter continued to gaze into the dimming light, wishing she were dead and only vaguely noticing the signposts she had so eagerly anticipated on her way to town. She was aroused from her reverie by the sound of a horse being ridden at speed on the road behind them. Looking back, she saw a cloud of dust. Someone was clearly in a hurry, but that was too common for it to occasion in her any more than a cursory interest. She heard the horseman coming closer, and braced herself to see him overtake. To her surprise, instead of overtaking at once, the rider seemed instead to deliberately stay abreast of their coach. Looking out indignantly to see who could be indulging in such dangerous behavior, her eyes met others, well known to her.

The commotion had Mr. Needwood stirring in his seat, and his eyes flew open. When he had earlier closed them, his daughter had been pale and listless. He was unprepared to see her newly animated, and with a glow of expectation on her cheeks.

"My dear girl, whatever is going on?" he said, puzzled, as he felt their coach slacken. "Why are we stopping?"

"I . . . I think it is Lord Markham," said Eleanor, suddenly very prim and innocent, sitting back against the squabs with her hands folded demurely in her lap.

"Lord Markham? Good Lord. Did you forget something, Nell?"

"I don't think so, sir," said his daughter, struggling to keep her face sensible, while all the time a fierce joy was bubbling up inside to make her feel like laughing.

"We had better see what he wants, then," said her father, beginning to have a suspicion that perhaps he already knew.

Lord Markham could now be seen through the window, and a few moments later was leaning across the sill to speak to Mr. Needwood. Gone was his immaculate town look. His greatcoat was covered in dust, and his boots splashed with mud.

"Forgive my dirt, sir," he said with his disarming smile. "I've been dashing, rather. Did you think it was highwaymen?"

"My daughter did not, at all events," said Eleanor's father, dipping his head in her direction. "She has not left her trunk behind?"

"Good Lord, no."

"Then . . . ?"

Lord Markham appeared suddenly less confident. He looked tentatively across at Eleanor. "I think, sir, that your daughter and I have things to say to each other."

Mr. Needwood looked from one to the other, and said to his daughter, "Is that so, Nell?"

Eleanor, who had been too embarrassed to lift her eyes to Lord Markham, did so now, and saw such tenderness there that she was flooded with happiness. "Yes, Father," she whispered, "I think we have."

"I'll give you ten minutes, then, sir. Not a moment longer, else the light'll be gone before we get to Northampton."

234

Lord Markham took hold of Eleanor's arm, handed her down from the coach, and led her to a nearby spinney. Her father tried not to look, but he could not prevent a smile when he saw her, some two minutes later, safely locked in Lord Markham's arms. Pretending not to notice his daughter's quite reprehensible behavior on the king's highway, he settled down in the corner, hat over his eyes, to await their return, thanking heaven that he was spared the arduous task of explaining to his wife how his daughter had rejected a marquess. And if anyone ever tried to tell him that there wasn't a God, he would know how to answer!